SLICE

SLICE

JUICY MOMENTS FROM MY IMPOSSIBLE LIFE!

STEVEN HERRICK

WOOLSHED PRESS
An Imprint of Random House Australia

A Woolshed Press book
Published by Random House Australia Pty Ltd
Level 3, 100 Pacific Highway, North Sydney NSW 2060
www.randomhouse.com.au

First published by Woolshed Press in 2010

Woolshed Press is a trademark of Random House Australia Pty Ltd.
All rights reserved.
www.woolshedpress.com.au

Addresses for companies within the Random House Group can be found at
www.randomhouse.com.au/offices.

Australian Government | **Australia Council** for the Arts

This project has been assisted by the Australian Government through the Australia Council, its arts funding and advisory body.

National Library of Australia
Cataloguing-in-Publication Entry

Author: Herrick, Steven
Title: Slice : juicy moments from my impossible life / Steven Herrick
ISBN: 978 1 86471 964 2 (pbk.)
Target Audience: For secondary school age
Subjects: Adolescence – Juvenile fiction
    Teenage boys – Juvenile fiction
Dewey Number: A823.3

Cover photography by Carole Gomez
Cover design by Mathematics, www.xy-1.com
Internal design by Midland Typesetters, Australia
Typeset in 12.5/16.25 pt Adobe Jenson Pro by Midland Typesetters, Australia
Printed and bound by Griffin Press, an Accredited ISO AS/NZS 14001:2004 Environmental Management System printer

10 9 8 7 6 5 4 3 2 1

SLICE

Darcy

My name is Darcy Franz Pele Walker.

Ignore the middle names.

I do.

My Dad is a football nut and he figured if he named me after his two favourite players, I'd turn out just like them. At the age of five, I'd stand in the backyard wearing baggy blue shorts and a Brazilian jersey watching the clouds, the trees, birds tilting overhead on the breeze.

Dad would shout, 'Ready, Darcy?' and roll the ball temptingly my way.

'Just kick it with all you've got, son.'

I'd look at the coloured panels on the ball.

'Just swing your foot, Darcy.'

Arms extended, I'd obediently sway my right leg like a ballerina stretching.

The football experiment stopped at age eleven. Years of frustration got the better of Dad and he belted one, straight at me. Bloodcurdling screams rent the suburb.

Not from me, from Mum.

I lay on my back, a warm ooze of blood trickling down my face.

People say I look better with a broken nose.

It's a slight lump.

You can hardly notice it.

Dad was distraught. Mum shouted at him for hours, bad language bouncing off the kitchen walls.

Dad said I'd never have to play football again.

I almost hugged him, but I didn't want to get blood all over his clean shirt.

Pele is some Brazilian dude, the greatest player of all time. When he retired he became the Minister for Sport in the Brazilian government. He did a television commercial for men with erection problems.

Franz is Franz Beckenbauer – the only person to win the World Cup as player and a coach. In his heyday he had a haircut like a laughing clown, curls framing an amiable, round, chubby face.

A normal sixteen-year-old

There are two minutes and twenty-four seconds until lunchtime.
Maths with Mr Clegg.
How's that for a name?
Caleb Clegg.

Some parents should be forbidden from naming their children.

Are you listening, Mum and Dad?

Mr Clegg is wearing a paisley shirt and mustard slacks with matching cowdung-coloured shoes. He has a sergeant-major haircut, lacquered down with Brylcreem (I saw it on his desk yesterday). According to Google, Brylcreem was used by old men and rock stars last century. It's made of beeswax.

Anyway, Wax-head is lecturing us on the relevance of Maths in daily life. He spouts forth (*spouts forth* — my attempt at Shakespeare) and he doth complain too much about nobody recognising the value of numeracy.

I won't bore you with the details. He's been raving for forty-three minutes and . . . fifteen seconds nonstop. We've been promised our final exam results today but I don't like our chances. The clock ticks down to one minute and thirty seconds until freedom. Stacey Scott slumps forward like an old lady nodding off over her knitting. If Clegg notices he'll keep us in after the bell.

I jump up from my desk, a finger pointing accusingly towards the clock. 'Sir. The time!'

Stacey bounces awake. Mr Clegg gasps, glasses hanging loosely off his broken nose. We have something in common!

'Darcy Walker, how dare you . . .'

'Sir, a quick calculation tells me we only have one minute left before lunch. You're right. Maths is useful!'

Sniggering comes from the losers in the back row. Gutless wonders!

4

'If you give us our results now, we'll see how relevant Maths will be in the future, won't we?'

Clegg sweeps his hand over his Brylcreem-stiff hair, mutters under his breath, then reaches for the results folder and walks to the front of his desk. I stand triumphantly waiting to be mobbed by cheering students, blokes slapping me on the back, girls offering kisses and seductive text messages.

Instead, Marcus Guyotus whines from the corner, 'Can you sit down, Darcy. I can't see the board.'

'There's nothing on the board, Marcus.'

'How do I know that, if you're in the way?'

'Open your eyes!'

'Sir, Walker just insulted me!'

'Telling somebody to open their eyes is not an insult, Marcus. Your haircut, on the other hand . . .'

'Walker! It's bad enough you interrupt me, it's worse you continue to hold the floor.'

'I'm technically not "holding" the floor, sir. I don't believe that's physically possible. All I'm . . .'

'Sit!'

I make like a dog and do as he commands.

The bell rings and everyone scrapes their chairs back in unison. Stacey is almost at the door when Clegg calls, 'Not so fast, sleepyhead. Walker demanded your results . . .' Clegg smiles. '. . . Something for you all to savour over lunch.'

Like a funeral bell tolling, he slowly reads our scores.

Nobody says a word, failures scatter like dead leaves.

Me?

61%!

Miranda and Stacey stand in the canteen line, Miranda's voice is like a chainsaw cutting through soft timber. 'Clegg is a prick. I can't believe he failed me. All Maths teachers are sadists. You'd have to be to . . .'

Stacey interrupts, 'Did he really say "sleepyhead"? Isn't there a rule against name-calling?'

Mrs Harrison, the canteen lady, drums her fingers on the bench waiting for them to order.

My stomach rumbles and my ears ache from listening to these two.

I lean forward. 'It's called bullying, but I'm not sure if "sleepyhead" qualifies.'

Miranda sneers, 'How would you know? Stacey is very sensitive. Aren't you Stace?'

'Please don't call me Stace.'

'See!'

Mrs Harrison rolls her eyes. 'Pies or sausage rolls. That's all we've got left.'

Miranda says, 'I'll have a salad sandwich.'

I'm sixteen years old and my mouth runs ahead of my brain. Our friend Pele would describe it as – ahem – premature enunciation. Mum says I talk without thinking. She's wrong.

I mean what I say, I just shouldn't say it aloud.

My parents

I drop my backpack on the floor in the kitchen and grab a bottle of juice from the fridge, shaking it so all the gunky stuff mixes with the ungunky stuff. In the lounge, Dad is reading the sports section with his feet up on the stool. It's the last day of his week-long break from work. He's an accountant.

'How was your day, Darcy?'

'Great. I had a cold pie for lunch and came second in my Maths exam.'

'Brilliant! What did you score?'

'Second in the class. I just told you.'

Dad folds the newspaper and rubs his hand over a six-day growth.

'What percentage?'

'You accountants are so concerned with figures. What about ranking? I repeat, "second-highest".'

Dad laughs. 'Just tell me you got over fifty per cent, Darcy.'

I slap his bare feet as I walk past to my bedroom. 'Your son is a success!'

Whenever Dad has a week or two off work, he grows a beard and contemplates his reflection in the mirror. He strolls around the neighbourhood, rubbing his whiskers like a homeless philosopher. He wears his shirt untucked with baggy shorts and leather sandals. Once I saw him outside a tattoo parlour admiring the designs in the window. He wandered over to the Harley parked outside and ran his hand lovingly over the leather seat. He dreams of rebellion while driving our Camry.

Until . . .

Tonight Mum has cooked spaghetti marinara, Dad's favourite.

Mum scoops huge helpings into each bowl while Dad opens the wine.

She rinses the saucepan in the sink and before sitting down, leans in close and kisses Dad. As she pulls away, her fingers linger on his stubble. 'Growing a beard, darling?'

Dad wriggles uncomfortably. 'Maybe.'

Mum makes a sound in the back of her throat.

Dad looks hurt. 'What?'

'Nothing, darling. It's just ...'

'You look good, Dad. Like a university dropout, or an artist.'

Mum takes a sip of wine. 'As I was saying ...' She glances at me. 'It's just ... well ... how many prime ministers have beards?'

'I'm an accountant, dear.'

'Tasty dinner, Mum.'

There's that sound in the back of her throat again. 'Trust, David. Clients demand trust.'

'A beard doesn't mean I'll take their investments and spend them on cocaine or gambling or wild women?'

'That'd be great, Dad.'

Mum raises her eyebrows.

'Not the wild women, Mum. Just the drugs and ...'

'Darcy, you are not helping matters.'

'I'm a teenager.'

'That's not an excuse.'

Dad sadly loops the spaghetti over his fork. Mum leans across and fills up his wine glass. The condemned beard's last drink.

When it turned out I didn't have the ball skills of Franz and Pele, Dad decided to play football himself. Every Sunday afternoon during winter, he drives twenty kilometres to compete in an over-35 men's competition. He didn't join the local club because he wanted to keep it a secret, in case he'd forgotten how to play.

As it turns out, Dad is a half-decent striker. Something to do with *failed childhood dreams manifesting themselves as an adult reality.* That's Dad, not Shakespeare. Mum and me almost choked on our lasagne when he said that over dinner after his first trial game.

In the following season, he scored eighteen goals and broke his left wrist in the last game.

Was he worried about the plaster?

No way. He was pleased it happened during the last game, so he'd have the off-season to heal.

Mum muttered darkly about future injuries.

Dad let me sign his cast.

On Saturday, when most dads are washing the car, pruning the hedge or mowing the lawn, Dad sits on the back step polishing his football boots. He gives me pass-by-pass accounts of his previous game, going into every detail of each shot, tackle, run. I allow him the dignity of thirty minutes reliving his last game. I'm sure he's tempted to run around the yard with a ball trying to recreate each game.

Mum would tell him to mind the roses and not make so much noise.

Dad should have been a professional footballer. Or a sports journalist. Not an accountant. An accountant without a beard.

Mum is a barrister. And she dresses like one. Lots of linen suits, silk blouses, black stockings and pointy shoes; crisp, expensive Italian style. A severe haircut that Dad calls a barrister-bob. A dark leather briefcase. No handbag – handbags are for girls. Mum's a power woman out to bring justice to the world.

I've sat in court watching her handling a case. She argues as if the future of the planet depends on the decision. Her whole body is energised as she strides between her desk and the front of the court. The click of her heels keep time with her loud and forceful voice. I'm expecting her to leap over the judge's box, grab him by the throat and shake him until he agrees.

That's Mum on the outside.

At home, she wears trackies and an old sweater. She washes all the make-up off and becomes a different woman. Kind and thoughtful and concerned and sincere.

It's like living with your school counsellor!

She has this habit of listening with such an intensity that sometimes I can't stop talking. I'm driven to fill the silence with an overdose of verbal slush. The more I go on, the closer she leans.

I've blurted out heaps of needless confessions on not finishing school assignments; of drinking at Stacey's parties; of deliberately being late for class when we've got Information Technology.

Maybe all mums are able to find out what they want, whenever they want.

It's a skill passed down from mother to daughter.

Fathers and sons?

Nah.

Just a desire to kick a ball or grow a beard.

Five things my dad told me not to do

Dad dearly wanted me to play football.
No luck.
  Now for the things he discouraged.
  Five, in particular.

What would you do if your dad told you not to do something?

Number One: SHAVE

Last term I noticed long dark soft hair sprouting from above my top lip. I stroked it and rubbed Mum's moisturiser in to encourage growth. The sooner I became a man the better. I half-expected Audrey Benitez, girl of my dreams in English class, to approach me at lunchtime and offer herself.

Finally, a man among minors!

The blokes at school kept asking when I was going to remove the caterpillar.

Adrian Vaughn in Art class called me Frida Kahlo.

Tim Harris used Stacey Scott's eyeliner to draw a moustache on himself. He yelled across the room before Maths began, 'Look, I'm just like Walker.'

I answered, 'You'd need to grow a penis first!'

Harris scowled and shoved his chair back, knocking Marcus's neatly arranged pens on the floor. Marcus looked distraught, leaning down to pick them up and toppling off his chair in the process. Stacey giggled. Tim wasn't sure if she was laughing at my joke or Marcus.

Mr Clegg walked in and told Tim to go wash his face. He looked at Marcus still on the floor and rolled his eyes. Harris brushed past my desk, whispering, 'Dead man, Walker.'

'But with a penis!' I shot back.

Clegg exploded. 'Walker, did you just swear?'

'"Pens", sir. I was worried about Marcus losing his "pens".'

At home, I ask Dad if I can borrow his razor.

A look of horror crosses his face.

'Sit down, son. We should have a chat.'

He pats the lounge, folds the newspaper and makes room for me.

He leans sideways. 'How long have you been having these thoughts, Darcy?'

'All week. Every time I look in the mirror.'

Dad winces and takes a deep breath.

'It's okay to be a little concerned about looks when you're young, son.'

He laughs to himself. 'I was convinced my nose was too long and thin when I was your age.'

He pats my knee. 'You'll grow out of it.'

I have no idea what he's talking about.

'So you'll give me a razor?'

'Darcy, suicide is . . .'

'. . . when someone ends it all. I know, Dad. I just want to shave!'

The tension releases from his body.

'I thought you meant . . .' His eyes cloud over. He smiles and leans forward, a look of utter false sincerity on his face, 'Don't do it, Darcy.'

Maybe I chose the wrong time for a chat? The newspaper is open at the football section. *Australia qualify for the World Cup* trumpets the headline.

'I want to shave, Dad. Not kill myself.'

He flinches at the word 'kill'.

'Yes, I know. But, don't do it.'

'Why?'

'Because once you start, you'll never be able to stop.'

Are we talking about masturbation, or shaving?

'I started when I was your age, Darcy. It was fun – for a while. I felt like a man. But then, every second day, I had to waste my time in front of the bathroom mirror.'

I'm a teenager. I'm supposed to waste time in front of mirrors! And shout obscenities at pensioners in shopping malls. And ride skateboards over stairs outside public libraries.

Dad sighs. 'And when you get a job like mine, you'll have to shave every day.'

An accountant! I'm never becoming ... The words are on the tip of my tongue.

'Come on, Dad.'

He picks up the paper, a picture of the Australian team celebrating under a huge banner.

I stand there, waiting.

Dad sighs. 'I'll buy you a razor tomorrow.'

It's amazing how much blood can come from such a tiny cut. Maybe I'll tell Tim Harris I got into a fight with a gang from another suburb and they cut me with a knife. Slashed across the chin but I still pummelled them. All four of those razor-wielding skateboard-riding acne-covered maniacs from Blackheath.

Number Two: DRINK

Every parent tells their offspring not to drink alcohol, usually over dinner as they pour themselves a glass of wine.

'It's dangerous. It impairs your judgement. It's bad for your health.'

Dad's stomach expands over his trousers and I wonder if I should carry a hidden tape recorder to play back when he's senile in an old people's home, a brown woollen blanket covering his knees as he sits in threadbare pyjamas on the garden seat and I'm enduring one of my monthly visits.

Dad takes another sip and reads the label.

'Twelve per cent alcohol. Do you know how much damage that can do to a young liver, son.'

What? His liver has developed an immunity!

Mum quickly adds, 'We're not perfect examples, dear. I had a glass of beer on my eighteenth birthday and didn't touch another drop until I met your father.'

'Meeting Dad *drove* you to drink?'

Dad finishes his glass and reaches for the bottle, then thinks better of it.

'Look, son. On your eighteenth. We'll have a big party to celebrate. You can have a few then.'

Mum and Dad feel confident promising things that won't happen in the next year. They hope I'll forget. But I have all my brain cells. I haven't destroyed them with alcohol.

Not yet!

Number Three: VOMIT

No, Dad didn't tell me I wasn't allowed to vomit 'ever'. Just not last Saturday night at midnight, in the Camry, on the way home from Stacey Scott's party. I'd drunk too much punch. It was a lovely shade of pink.

No-one told me there was alcohol in it.

No-one told me there was too much alcohol in it.

No-one told me I shouldn't drink six glasses of the stuff.

Stacey had mixed one part cranberry juice to two parts vodka. She said it was a healthy alternative.

Dad looked quickly over his shoulder when I groaned, just in time to yell, 'Darcy. Don't vomit!'

I would have been more than happy to obey him. Alas, a pink fountain spurted from my mouth all over the leather upholstery.

I bet Shakespeare never wrote a line like that!

I'll repeat it.

Alas, a pink fountain spurted from my mouth all over the leather upholstery.

Incidentally, I learnt something interesting about toads yesterday. When they've eaten something really toxic, they vomit up their entire stomach, not just the food. They use their right arm to remove the toxic meal from their stomach lining. Once it's clean, they swallow their stomach again.

On Sunday, I used a mop, bucket and twenty-five paper towels to clean up the mess.

I understand why the word 'chunky' is often used in the same sentence as 'vomit'.

See, I just did it then.

That's the last time I'm drinking this month.

It's August 28th.

Number Four: FIGHT FAIR

It would have been much easier if Dad told me not to fight, no matter what the circumstance. I could have said to Tim Harris that I'd love to beat him to a pulp, but, you know, I promised my dad.

Dad is one of these old-school types who think part of manhood is fighting honourably. He'd prefer Tim and I wear boxing gloves. To go three rounds in the school gym. No low blows.

It didn't work out like that.

You wouldn't even call it a fight. It was an unfortunate disagreement.

Tim pushed in front of me in the canteen line.

Yes, this is high school, not kindergarten.

Normally, I wouldn't care. Anyone eager to eat canteen food deserves all they get. But as Tim muscled his way in, I saw Audrey glance our way.

Being only a few thousand years removed from my cave-man ancestors, I pushed him and yelled, 'Hey!'

Normally, that would have been it.

Except Tim was leaning forward and he fell, face first, at the feet of Audrey.

Note: I'd be quite happy to fall at the feet of Audrey.

But, for footy-Tim this was 'a loss of face'. No, he didn't have his face smeared across the concrete. It's a metaphor.

Tim jumped up quickly and threw a punch, roughly in my direction.

I dodged his fist much better than I dodged the soccer ball when I was a kid. His fist missed me . . . and hit the side wall.

I dearly wanted to yell something suitably antagonistic like, 'Try again, Tim. The wall didn't fall over.'

Tim was still holding his damaged fist when the canteen lady called, 'Next!'

This was too much, even for me.

'Please, Tim. You go first. You can eat it on the way to hospital.'

Anyway, to cut a long and embarrassing story short, Harris jumped on me and we rolled around on the concrete together, him swearing and trying to throw a punch with his good hand, me clinging on for dear life. Maybe it looked like I had him in a macho bear hug, vigorously squeezing the life out of him?

If I were a toad, boy, my guts would have jumped right out all over Harris.

People describe our principal, Mrs Archer, as a 'consensus type'.

Tim and I were quite willing to agree to hate one another. Mrs Archer wanted us to apologise *and* shake hands. Tim reluctantly held out his good left hand, I extended my right hand. We stood in Archer's office, trying to work out how to shake. I compromised and offered my left. Tim gripped tightly, wanting to snap my wrist.

'Fighting never gets you anywhere.'

Mrs Archer didn't expect an answer.

Inside I was screaming, *It's got Tim to hospital!!!*

'Do I have your agreement this antagonism will cease?'

Tim answered, 'No, Mrs Archer.'

'What!'

'She means, we should stop fighting, Tim.'

Harris scowled at me. 'I know what she said.'

Mrs Archer rose abruptly from her chair, her face red and flushed.

'Stop saying "she" in my presence!

'If you boys fight again, it will result in suspension!'

So much for consensus.

I quickly answered, 'Yes, Mrs Archer,' just in case Tim got confused again.

Mrs Archer fired a few more verbal arrows our way then sent me back to class and Tim to the doctor.

Sprained, not broken.

Number Five: MASTURBATE

No parent in their right mind wants to discuss . . . self-love, shall we say, but . . .

Do you know the newsreader on SBS? She's got lustrous dark hair and skin the colour of coffee – latte, not cappuccino. She wears elegant low-cut blouses and shiny silver necklaces and, instead of listening to her report on the fighting in Afghanistan or the floods in China, sometimes my focus wanders.

Or becomes a little too obsessive.

She smiles in between segments and sometimes, before speaking, she takes a long breath, her shoulders lifting imperceptibly. It's a short walk from the troubles of the world on SBS to my bedroom.

I should have locked the door.

Dad should have knocked.

Mercifully, it was a quick conversation. Dad told me to 'limit the activity'.

And I do.

The teenager on the roof

My parents have an amazing bedroom.

They climb a ladder in the lounge room and push open a little trapdoor through the floor to enter their loft.

I thought only poets lived in lofts – alone with their fountain pens and bad haircuts, writing about trees and rivers before dying young of misadventure or some incurable disease.

Did you know that Shelley, the Romantic poet, drowned in a boating accident off the coast of Italy? He was twenty-nine years old. He and two friends were enjoying a quick sail across the water when a sudden storm blew up.

Romantics couldn't swim and refrained from wearing life jackets.

What would an eighteenth-century life jacket look like? Maybe a pig's bladder, leftover from an opulent banquet in a medieval castle, inflated by some poor peasant and strapped to your back with twine.

When Shelley's body washed ashore, it was burnt on the beach in a funeral pyre.

Before cremation, his heart was removed by a friend and given to his wife who kept it with her until she died. His poetry became even more famous, only he was too dead to reap the benefits.

Dad taught me to swim when I was ten.

Every Saturday morning at the pool, Dad stood in chest-deep water holding both my hands, dragging me forward, telling me to stick my head under the water and blow. I learnt quickly because I was embarrassed holding Dad's hand in public.

Mum and Dad were hippies long before I was born and they promised each other when they got married, they'd sleep in a loft, their bed pushed close to the window.

If you open their bedroom window and remove

the flyscreen, you can climb out onto the roof and look out over the whole suburb and the distant cliffs in the National Park.

When I was a kid, me and Dad would sit up here for hours and he'd tell stories about climbing trees, tree houses and birdwatching when he was young.

I can see everything up here on the roof.

To be more precise, I can see Audrey Benitez's back garden.

Audrey is the most beautiful girl in school.

There are more popular girls.

Girls that Tim Harris would eloquently describe as 'hotter'.

Miranda Fry.

Claire Rusina.

Stacey Scott.

They are not Audrey.

Let me describe her.

Mid-length oil-black hair. Not curly, just full and heavy. You want to touch it and see if any of the shine rubs off on your fingers. It never looks combed.

Permanently messy and amazingly beguiling. I just swapped the word 'attractive' for 'beguiling' – it has a nice ring to it. I love my thesaurus.

Audrey has slightly crooked teeth. When she smiles, you can't help but smile back because those teeth seem to have a life of their own. They ask you to join in on the fun.

Olive skin? No. The only olives I know are green. Audrey does not have green skin. It's smooth and . . . skin-coloured. Kind of dark beige, I guess.

What makes Audrey special is her eyes.

Brown and bright, they look at you and seem to be talking.

They're expressive.

When Tim Harris sprawled at her feet in the canteen line, the thing that gave me the most pleasure was not pushing Cro-Magnon man over, it was seeing the look of pity and scorn in Audrey's eyes as she looked down at him. Her eyes penetrate deep into you. She has a bright future as a psychotherapist.

As for the rest of Audrey?

She has two legs that seem quite nice to me. And hips and breasts. She's not fat. Or thin. She has no visible deformities. She doesn't have a nervous twitch, no Tourette syndrome, she's not given to spitting in public or excessive displays of hugging or screaming or saying 'Oh my God'.

She doesn't sit on warm concrete at lunchtime.
She's sixteen and I love her.
Okay!
There. I've said it.
So, let's move on with my life.

I'm lying on my back up on the roof.

The sun warms the corrugated iron and radiates through my whole body. Spider-web clouds move east towards the city on the breeze.

In the cedar tree beside the house, a white cockatoo pulls apart cones with his beak to eat the seed inside. When he finishes each cone he squawks, as if to say, 'How's that!'

Audrey walks out the back door of her house and stretches a mat across the grass in her garden. She's wearing black tights and a dark close-fitting sweater, her hair is pulled tight and tied in a short ponytail.

She looks like a spy from a 1960s James Bond movie.
She sits, lotus position.

A little bead of sweat trickles down my temple.

She places her hands on her knees, palms facing out.

My hands are fist tight, the veins bulging on my wrist.

She lifts her chin and takes a long slow deep breath.

I sigh.

Every afternoon, Audrey meditates. And I . . .

She looks up quickly, through the gap in the trees towards our house.

I duck.

Did she see me?

Maybe I should have waved, acted like I'm meditating as well. Sure I'm very interested in Indian mysticism, Tai Chi and your body.

I mean, Tai Chi and yoga.

The bead of sweat on my temple is joined by one hundred and twenty-four cousins, all scampering down to drop sizzling onto the hot tin roof.

How long should I stay hidden?

Dad pops his head out of the window.

'What on earth are you doing, son?'

Perving on Audrey Benitez! What does it look like!

'Nothing, Dad.'

'Nothing can come of nothing.'

'Is that Shakespeare?'

Dad rolls his eyes. 'Just don't fall off. Okay?'

He slides the window closed, but doesn't lock it.

Maybe you think I am perving on Audrey?

I prefer to think of it as fifteen minutes of admiring great art.

Fifteen minutes of quiet time.

Fifteen minutes of sharing something with the woman of my dreams.

Even if she doesn't know it yet.

I raise my head slightly, peeking over the gutter. Audrey is sitting, motionless. I can hear the faintest drone.

A jumbo passing overhead?

Or Audrey doing Yoga Sound Meditation?

I read about it on the web. You release all the air slowly from your upper lung, followed by the middle lung and then the lower one. I never knew my lungs had three storeys. Audrey is so exceptional, her lungs probably have four storeys. And a loft.

The sexual history of Darcy Walker

I am leaning against the kitchen sink at Stacey Scott's monthly party. Her dad is away on a business trip (on the weekend?) and her mum is floating off to a health resort 'to get her head together'. How do I know that? Because Mrs Scott hasn't left yet. The two of us are alone in the kitchen.

Stacey's mum points a bright red fingernail. 'With me away, it gives Stacey time to explore her,' she tosses back her hair, 'personality.'

'Personality?'

'Her . . . sexuality, if you like.'

There are words parents should not be allowed to say in the company of teenagers. 'Sexuality' is high up on the list. Along with 'condoms', 'orgasm', and 'homework'.

I study the wonderful array of wine glasses on the counter behind Mrs Scott.

She has hair the colour of ripe wheat. Her lips seem too big for her face. They could suck all the oxygen out of the kitchen if she inhaled deeply.

I should answer, 'Yes, Mrs Scott. At our age, Stacey and I need all the exploring we can get.'

Or . . .

'That's an enlightened response. Would you care to have a word with my parents sometime?'

Instead . . .

'Did . . . did . . . did you paint those fingernails yourself?'

Mrs Scott holds up both hands, slowly blows on each of the nails, causing a mini-tornado to sweep around the room. 'They're still wet and,' she steps closer –

'I did my toes as well.'

To look down would be fatal. I call over her shoulder to Marcus Guyotus, who is imitating a statue on the verandah.

Marcus, my saviour! Tonight, you have a friend.

Marcus and I talk about the pyramids of Egypt and how the Pharaohs took their slaves to the grave with them. Thirty years being a servant for some born-to-rule dude and when he finally carks it, your reward is to sit beside his dead body in a vault.

I'd be indulging in serious corpse mutilation while waiting for the hereafter, the word 'Dickhead' scrawled across my ruler's forehead.

When I'm sure Mrs Scott has left, I go back to the kitchen, leaving Marcus to ancient history and the cruel death of Agamemnon.

The rugger types like Tim Harris and Braith Miller are hogging the lounge room, where they can control the music and dance with as many girls as possible. They'll end up drinking far too much, singing really ugly beer-sculling songs and slamming into each other in a poor imitation of a mosh pit.

It's like a replay of the afternoon footy game.

I prefer the kitchen, the source of food and drink.

All first dibs to me.

Miranda is pouring a large amount of vodka into the blender while Stacey is cutting up a watermelon. Vodka and watermelon? What is it with Stacey and pink liquid?

She's wearing a black leather mini-skirt coupled with white stockings. Up top, she's wearing a black bra with silver tassels attached. They bounce as she dances, threatening to take out the eye of anyone who ventures too close. Her hair is peroxide fresh.

Miranda has gone goth. Too much black is never enough, particularly around the eyes. She looks like a startled panda. Her boots are black and shiny and have clunky soles that make dancing a high-wire balancing act.

Stacey and Miranda pour two glasses and drink it down quickly. Their faces go red. Stacey lets out a loud 'whoa' before they both bend over double, giggling and holding each other up. When they straighten, Stacey looks at Panda-girl and says, 'Too much watermelon!'

Remembering my history with pink liquid, I pass on the offer of a cocktail glass and walk outside where Marcus is talking to a girl.

I'll repeat that.

Marcus is talking to a girl.

They both lean over the railing as far as possible. Marcus points to the sky.

'You can see his belt. Just there. Four stars left of the moon.'

If I had such amusing interests, the opposite sex might talk to me at parties.

The girl doesn't go to our school. She's wearing a tight, short dress with blood-red stockings and knee-high boots. She's dyed the front locks of her fringe to match the stockings.

Marcus giggles excitedly. 'It's mega bright this time of the year.'

The girl grips tightly to the railing. 'It's called Ryan?'

'Orion, the hunter. He fought Scorpio.'

All of a sudden, the girl turns around and stumbles into my arms.

I know Marcus can be boring, but to knock them out with facts about the planets is some achievement.

The girl grips both my shoulders and pulls herself upright.

I mumble, 'Sorry,' for no particular reason.

She looks from me to Marcus, back to me, then closes her eyes and starts kissing me. I mean really kissing me. Open-mouth, tongue-dancing, arms-around-my-waist, bodies-touching kissing.

What can I do?

I kiss back.

The chaotic aroma of vodka and perfume tickles my nostrils.

As we kiss, her fingernails dig into my ribcage. I risk opening my eyes.

Marcus is standing close behind her, waving his arms and saying, 'But ... but ... what about Orion?'

The girl doesn't seem interested in Orion, the moon, or Scorpio. She's attached to me like a vacuum to a rug.

I'm not complaining, just confused.

Is my animal magnetism that strong?

Has she been spying on me for ages, like I've been watching Audrey?

Or is she trying to escape the monumental boredom of a Guyotus astronomy lecture?

And then she burps.

While we're kissing.

Probably a lack of air. Just a timid stomach movement? A reflex?

She reels back from me, pushes Marcus out of

the way and vomits over the verandah. The sound is bone-shakingly loud.

Everyone in the lounge room stops dancing and braces themselves, fearing an earthquake rumbling underneath.

Stacey and Miranda are already under the table, finishing off the contents of the blender, so they're safe from falling lampshades and broken glass.

A technicolour hailstorm gushes over the railing.

I move tentatively beside her and put my hand on her shoulder.

Marcus gets up, dusts himself down and points a finger accusingly at me. 'A girl kisses you, Walker, and then throws up.'

He marches inside with an insanely conceited grin on his face.

When Marcus Guyotus feels superior to me at a party, it's time to leave.

I offer to call the girl a taxi.

Shakespeare would say her eyes are great pools of sadness. Truth is they're bloodshot, smudged with eyeliner and out of focus. She vomits forcefully again.

I take that as a no.

It's a long, agonising walk home. Marcus is right about one thing. Orion is very clear in the eastern sky.

My favourite school subject

Our school has eighty-four students in Year Eleven.

Twelve are studying Advanced English, the rest are doing Standard and struggling. Tim and Braith almost got into a fight with the careers advisor at the end of last year when he told them they had to choose one English subject or the other. They couldn't drop English altogether. Braith's response was prophetic.

'We don't need English!'

No-one giggled, not even the girls.

The advisor spoke carefully. 'Sorry, Braith. Government policy, I'm afraid.'

Braith leant back in his chair, put his hands behind his head and sneered, 'Well, don't expect anything from me in class!'

The advisor suggested Braith do his best and looked mighty relieved when the bell rang.

Tim sulked. 'We're gunna go on strike all next year.'

The advisor packed his brochures into his bag and quickly left the room.

Braith and Tim stood at their desks as the rest of us filed out. They were shouting, 'Strike! Strike! Strike!'

It took them a few minutes to realise no-one was listening and it was lunchtime.

The Year Eight boy at the head of the canteen line let them in first.

Braith slid his money across the counter and pointed to a pie in the front rack of the oven to prove he didn't need English.

Or language of any kind.

English with Ms Hopkins is simply wonderful.

She has short, cropped hair, wears jeans and riding boots and has an endless supply of T-shirts with slogans and images. Today's shirt has a Soviet cosmonaut sailing above a hammer and sickle, with a slogan in Russian.

There are piles of books with funky covers on her desk, in the bookshelf, stacked haphazardly on the floor.

Anytime we want to take one home, it's fine by her.

She's a library service without the cards and date stamps and prying questions.

None of the books are set texts. All look well read and lived-in.

She encourages us to read whatever we want. You could bring a comic into class and within fifteen minutes she'd have us all discussing the homosexual subtext of Batman and Robin. Or looking at the semiotic relationship between the bat car and the bat cave and all those leather outfits.

It sounds like a wank, I know.

But she actually values our opinion on books. And not just what teachers expect you to say – you know, about images and metaphors-per-square-centimetre.

This week we're studying *Heart of Darkness*.

Ms Hopkins sits on her desk, holding the book in her hands, fingernails painted black. I can't resist. 'Did you paint your nails in theme, Ms?'

She studies her hands and smiles. 'Into the heart of darkness through nail polish, the horror. Did you finish it last night, Darcy?'

Everyone looks at me.

They expect me to rave about how deep and bleak and tragic it all is, to use words like *ominous* and *brooding*, to quote Shakespeare.

Ms Hopkins smiles, encouragingly.

I sigh. 'It's the longest one hundred and twenty-seven pages I've ever read, Ms. Doctors should prescribe it for insomniac patients. They'd be snoring in minutes.'

Miranda Fry giggles.

'Sorry, Ms. I know it's a classic, but I'd rather clean my room or mow the lawn or cut my toenails than read it again.'

Ms Hopkins laughs. 'It's okay, Darcy. By the end of class, I hope you'll change your mind.'

For the next forty-five minutes we talk about man's dark soul, the terrorism of 9/11, original sin, vanity and desire ... and do you know what? I still hate *Heart of Darkness* – and love Ms Hopkins for trying.

But what really focuses my attention all class is Audrey Benitez. In a group of twelve students, it's pretty obvious if one person doesn't say a word.

Just before the bell, not even Ms Hopkins can stand it any longer.

'Audrey, what do you think of Conrad's masterpiece?'

Audrey brushes her hair from her eyes, looks around at all the students, smiles at me and says, 'I agree with Darcy.'

I almost fall off my chair.

Ms Hopkins asks, 'And?'

Audrey says, 'I think *Heart of Darkness* sucks shit big time, Ms.'

I am in love.

As Audrey would say – big time!

The perfect lunchtime ... almost

Normally at lunch, I sit in the senior common room and talk to whoever is there. Sometimes I play chess with Noah Hennessy (aka 'Noah No-one') because no-one else will.

But not today.

I sit against the school fence, looking down at the oval where Tim and Braith stand forty metres apart, Tim holding a football.

Braith calls to him, 'Kick it as high as you can. Two bucks says I can catch it.'

'Bullshit!'

'Go on.'

'I ain't giving you two dollars.'

'Okay. A dollar then.'

'I ain't . . .'

'Just kick the ball, will ya!'

Tim gives Braith the finger, then boots it as hard as he can, straight up in the air. Braith stands his ground, hands on hips. They both watch as the ball sails, end over end, and lands behind Tim.

When it stops rolling, Tim calls, 'You owe me two dollars.'

'We didn't bet, dipstick. And you're supposed to kick it to me. Not backwards.'

Tim walks back to collect the ball. Braith calls, 'Two bucks says I can catch it.'

I close my eyes and think of Audrey in English class.

Never has bad language sounded so sweet.

'Hi.'

Wow! I must really have it bad. I can hear her voice, even in my head.

'Hi.'

There it is again. If only I could picture her as well.

Squeezing my eyes tightly shut, I concentrate with all I've got, picturing Audrey.

A tap on my shoulder and I open my eyes.

It's Audrey.

'Were you asleep?'

'Me. No, I was . . . I was daydreaming.'

Her body is a silhouette against the sun.

Please, no jokes about the sun shines out of Audrey.

She sits beside me, near enough for me to go dizzy with her scent.

Fresh soap and apple-fragrance shampoo.

'After everyone left, Ms Hopkins told me not to swear in class.'

Audrey smiles. In her left eye, deep in the iris where it's dark and brown, there's one little speck of green.

'Really?'

'Yep. Then she laughed and said it was the most succinct answer she'd heard all week.'

'She's cool.'

Audrey pushes herself back against the fence, statue straight.

'She's one reason I took Advanced.'

'What's the other?'

She nods towards the oval.

'A desperate need to escape the attentions of Braith bloody Miller.'

'No!'

She pulls a long slither of grass from the ground and tickles herself under the chin.

'Talk about sucking shit big time. I've even stopped going to Stacey's parties. He kept coming up and leaning all over me. Beer and sweat and aftershave.'

She wrinkles her nose.

I remember Dad offering me his aftershave. 'Brut 33?'

Audrey grimaces. 'Uurrrgghhh.'

'I don't wear aftershave. It rips into your skin and leaves a rash.'

Audrey reaches across and touches my chin, just lightly, feeling for prickles.

'What is it with men and facial hair? My cousin keeps checking himself in the mirror, stroking his chin. He's twelve years old! Is it boy-to-man stuff?'

'How else can we tell?'

Audrey turns quickly to face me, staring with those brown eyes, and the one speck of green.

'Really? You don't know when you're a man?'

'Well . . . it's pretty complicated, don't you think?

'Not that you're a man, Audrey.

'It's just, who do we measure ourselves against? Our fathers?'

'Why compare yourself with anyone. Isn't being a man about standing alone?'

I've no idea what a man is. But it's a bit hard to admit that to the girl of my dreams.

Maybe I'd be better off with Noah in the common room, waiting for his next chess move. Noah rubs his right ear whenever he's about to make a seriously devious move.

'I don't know, Audrey. Bugger it. I don't want to be a man!'

Audrey grins, slowly. 'What do you want to be then?'

Say, 'Your boyfriend, Audrey.'

Stop shaking. She'll think you have a nervous twitch or you're one of those top-button nerds who loiter outside libraries, doing complicated maths equations in their head to pass the time.

Come on, say, 'Your boyfriend, Audrey.' It's three simple words.

'Happy.'

Phew. That was close.

'Happy?'

'Sure. Why not? If I'm happy, then whether I'm a man or an amoeba doesn't matter. Does it?'

'What's an amoeba?'

'No idea. Something small and insignificant.'

Audrey releases the scrunchy from her hair and shakes it loose.

I almost faint.

No, not because I go weak with her beauty. Although ...

Because, Tim 'Thick-neck' Harris miskicks the ball and it lands slap-bang on top of my head and bounces over the fence onto the footpath.

Audrey leans close, touching my scalp to check for damage.

It's all internal, Audrey.

Braith lumbers up the hill. 'Where's me ball?'

Audrey stands up and points at me, 'You could have hurt him!'

Braith looks at me, then at Audrey.

'So?'

'So you should try apologising, ya boofhead.'

I love that word *boofhead*. Especially when spoken by Audrey.

Braith sneers, 'To him?'

Does this prove my point about being a man?

Shouldn't I jump up and make Braith apologise? Isn't Audrey being more of a man than me? If I confront Braith, it'll end in another broken nose for me.

Humiliation.

Blood.

Torn shirt.

Bruises.

Followed by a visit to the principal's office with a letter home to the parents.

I got lucky last time with Tim. Braith is a much more dangerous creature. He stands looking from Audrey to me to the ball on the footpath.

I jump over the fence and run to the ball.

Tim has scrawled his name and address on it. So he'll remember where he lives?

I pick it up and walk back to the fence.

'Here, Braith.'

It's good to feel the smooth leather in my hands. It stops them shaking too much.

Audrey looks at me, pity and disappointment in her eyes.

My voice is pure nerd. 'Sorry my head got in the way of your ball, Braith. I'll try not to let it happen again.'

He grabs the ball and mutters, 'Yeah, well . . . watch it!'

He holds the ball high to show Tim he's found it, then trundles down the hill like a truck without a handbrake.

51

Audrey stares at me.

For good measure, I call to Braith, 'Let me know if I can fetch it again.'

I climb back over the fence and sit on the hard ground, waving to Braith even though he's turned away, holding the ball delicately in his hands, lining up another shot at the imaginary goal in his mind.

Audrey stands with her hands on her hips.

'What was that about?'

'I took your advice, Audrey.'

'Pardon?'

'You said a man should stand alone, know what he is, what he wants.'

Audrey looks at me as if the knock has tumbled my brain around a little too much.

I hold up one finger.

'Firstly, I'm not capable of fighting Braith. He'd kill me. There, I admit it.'

Two fingers.

'I'm not ashamed of avoiding a fight by jumping over the fence to get his ball. No skin off my nose.'

Three fingers.

'It was more fun to mess with his mind by agreeing with him then doing the obvious.'

Four fingers.

'Getting beaten up in front of you – there's nothing manly in that, is there?'

Five fingers.

'Mahatma Gandhi, Martin Luther King, Nelson Mandela, Darcy Walker – all non-violent revolutionaries!'

Audrey smiles with those perfectly crooked teeth. She steps closer and punches me, just lightly, on the arm.

'You big coward.'

'Call me Amoeba Man!'

Audrey steps in front of me, holding her arms wide in mock protection.

'Don't worry. I'll stand between you and Braith. Just in case he attacks.'

'Audrey, you're the man of my dreams.'

The English essay

I wrote about him because he's dead. You can write what you like about the dead and you won't get in trouble until you meet again in heaven, or hell – if you believe in that stuff. And what are they going to do? Kill you? Or send you back to earth, so they can ... kill you?

He was my grandfather. Dad's dad. Grandpa Stan. We visited him every Sunday morning when I was young. Only Dad and me went. Mum had work to catch up on. She always made me wear my best clothes – a neat white shirt with dark-blue stitching and the same trousers I'd worn to Aunt Alma's third wedding. Dad kept mentioning the word 'third' throughout the reception until Mum kicked him under the table, twice on the shin. He showed me the bruise when we got home. He was really drunk. He rolled up his trouser leg and asked me to take a photo. We were both giggling. Dad said, 'I'm going to frame it and give it to your mother on our next anniversary.'

Mum told me to hug Grandpa Stan when I arrived and before I left. To talk really loudly because he's deaf. To sit close and tell him all about school. To say 'please' and 'thank you' whenever he offered me a biscuit or a cordial. To keep my hands in my lap and not touch all the mementos in his house. My head was spinning trying to remember everything.

Me and Dad drove down the coast. I was excited because I got to sit in the front seat, watching Dad change gear, listening to him swear under his breath whenever another driver did something wrong. There was a plague of bad drivers on Sunday.

Grandpa lived near a freshwater lake, where he fished most days. His house was a tumbledown fibro shack. There was a sign over the front door, *Emoh*

Ruo. When we knocked, Grandpa would yell from the lounge room, 'Come in if ya good looking.'

Dad would call back, 'It's me.'

Grandpa would scratch his chin and say, 'Don't know anyone of that name.'

He'd take one long look at me and say, 'Have you been standing in fertiliser, my boy?'

I'd check the soles of my shoes.

He'd laugh, fit to burst.

'You've grown, young man.' Then he'd offer me chocolate biscuits on a tray. 'Here, have a dozen of these. They're good for your teeth.'

Dad would say, 'Don't listen to Grandpa, son. He's the world's best bull– Grandpa.'

'Thanks, Dave,' Grandpa would say. 'Now make yourself useful and get me a cup of tea, will you.'

Grandpa would wink at me. 'And get your son a cordial to wash down all these biscuits he's going to eat.'

Grandpa sat on a lounge chair in the corner of the room.

The chair had frayed edges, like a cat had been scratching.

The only other furniture was a coffee table, an old stereo and a long sideboard cluttered with photos, medals and ribbons that I was too scared to look at because I'd be tempted to touch them.

There was no television.

Grandpa had a sun-beaten, lined face with chins that jiggled when he laughed. His eyes were vivid pale blue and he winked constantly, as if letting you in on a joke, even when there wasn't one. His teeth grinned from a jar of water on the coffee table. He was always dressed in grey overalls with a flannelette shirt underneath. He wore tartan slippers and no socks.

He had a bald head, as shiny as a marble. I sat on the floor watching the light and shadows move across Grandpa's skull, wanting to touch it. After a while, I stopped listening to the conversation, focusing only on his head, mesmerised.

When he showered every night, did he wash it with extra-special soap?

Did he polish it with Vaseline, sewing-machine oil, clear boot polish?

Did it feel smooth and oily? Or soft?

When Grandpa wore a hat, did it blow off easily in the breeze?

When it was time to leave, I hugged Grandpa. His skin was soft. He smelt of eucalyptus and old leather. He said, 'You can touch my skull, young-un. No worries. As smooth as silk.'

He was right.

He'd give Dad a big hug and offer him a parcel wrapped in newspaper, 'a present for the missus.' When we got home, I'd unwrap it and find a whole freshwater bream, or prawns, or a crab.

Sunday dinner was my favourite.

Ms Hopkins wrote at the end of my essay that it was 'a wonderful portrait of a well-loved family member'.

Grandpa died years ago.

I wore the same clothes to his funeral.

On the first Sunday of every month, at daybreak, Dad drives to Grandpa's grave. He picks daisies from our garden and packs a broom to sweep the gravestone.

Once I followed him on my pushbike.

I hid behind a fig tree.

Dad stood at the foot of the grave.

It looked like he was talking – telling Grandpa about his week?

Occasionally, he'd reach up and brush away a fly from his face.

He stood very still for a long time.

Before leaving, he walked to the headstone and lightly touched the words. I leant against the tree and didn't move for ages. When I was sure no-one was around, I walked down to Grandpa's grave. His middle name was Darcy.

The marble was cool and smooth to touch. Just like Grandpa's bald head.

I didn't put that in the essay.

The school

It's the closest high school to my house. My parents are rich enough to send me to a private school, but they're still hippies at heart.

Mum said, 'We want you to have access to the full range of what society has to offer.' Dad almost choked on his tofu burger, then nodded his head in agreement.

Our uniform is grey pants, shirt and jumper. How's that for colour co-ordination! There's an unspoken competition among the boys to see who can wear their pants the lowest without getting sent to the principal. So far, Tim is winning.

The top of his pants are somewhere between his waist and his knees. He has to walk in very small steps to keep them from falling around his ankles. There's a daily increasing gap between shirt and trousers.

The underpant gap.

It's not a pretty sight.

Tim walks like a duck trying to be a homie! A duck with attitude! A duck pretending he's from the slums of New York. A football swaggering duck.

But still a duck . . .

The school motto is written in Latin: *Aliquando et insanire iucundum est.*

In English class, we tried guessing what it could mean.

Stacey suggested, 'To strive is a waste'.

Miranda, 'At lunchtime to sleep'.

Noah, 'All struggle in vain'.

Marcus, 'No paper in the toilets'!

My suggestion?

'Together whatever'.

Ms Hopkins knew, of course, but refused to divulge.

At Assembly after lunch, a local member of parliament visits to address the school. He wears a dark blue suit, his shoes are shined to perfection and his skin looks like he's spent too long under a sunlamp. He blathers on about modern technology and the value of a well-rounded education. Obviously, a speech he's delivered a thousand times without any changes.

Until the last line.

He flourishes his notes, turns towards the school motto above the stage curtain, and says, 'Young men and women, never forget your school motto . . .'. He stumbles over the pronunciation, coughs once, turns bright red and gestures for Mrs Archer to step forward and tell us what it means in English.

Eight hundred and ten students all lean forward, eager.

At last!

The meaning.

Mrs Archer strides across stage, shakes his hand vigorously and leads him away. They disappear through the curtain. The Deputy Principal, Mr Sloane, is left alone on stage, his hands behind his back, waiting. Praying, no doubt.

After a full two minutes of silence, he steps forward and says, 'Assembly dismissed.'

We file out of the hall.

Stacey says, 'Maybe that's what it means? *Assembly dismissed*.'

Miranda giggles.

During Information Technology class, I do the obvious and search the internet for Latin quotes, phrases and mottos.

Aliquando et insanire iucundum est means 'it is sometimes pleasant to act like a madman'.

My classmates

Stacey sits in the common room, chewing gum and texting. She rests her feet on the chair in front, her legs crossed at the ankles.

'Stacey?'

'No.'

'I haven't asked you anything!'

'No, I'm not having a party this weekend. Mum and Dad are home. And yelling at each other. I'm staying at Miranda's.'

She puts the mobile in her bag. 'I got in trouble because of all the vomit in the garden.'

'It wasn't me!'

Stacey rolls her eyes. As if I need reminding.

'Stacey, I'm doing some research for Society and Culture, on teenagers.'

'You mean us. Why do you need to research yourself?'

'Not just me. Other people.'

'Girls?'

'In one word, yes. So can I ask you some questions? All the data will be kept secret. Anonymous. Trust me.'

Stacey looks at her watch, but can't think of a good excuse to leave.

'Five questions only, Stacey. How's that?'

'Okay. But I'm not telling secrets. I promised Miranda.'

I try to ignore the obvious.

'Fair enough, let's start with school.'

Stacey groans and reaches for her mobile.

'Okay, forget school. How about food?'

'Easy. If it's green, it's good. If it's yellow, it's fattening.'

'And if it's black?'

'It's Coca-Cola, stupid.'

'Fair enough. How about drugs?'

Stacey looks quickly towards the door.

'How much?'

'What?'

'I'll need to take something to Miranda's. How much are you charging?'

'No. I mean, what is your view on drugs?'

'Oh.' She giggles. 'Just say no!'

'Come on, Stacey, it's anonymous, okay.'

She shrugs. 'Drugs are okay, I guess. Better than alcohol. Cheaper. Quicker.'

Stacey leans forward, takes the gum out of her mouth and sticks it to the strap of her schoolbag. It's pink in colour.

'Drugs are . . .' She searches the ceiling for the right word.

I offer, 'Cool?'

She keeps looking up, 'Much cheaper if you steal from your brother's stash.'

Stacey's brother is a gun athlete at university. I'm shocked he allows such impurities into his body. Whatever happened to the Olympian ideal? Drugs, of course.

'Stacey, what's your favourite music?'

She giggles, 'Loud. House. Dance. Electric folk. You name it.'

'Okay. What about sex?'

Stacey frowns. 'You want me to tell you about sex?'

She looks at me as if I've got a nasty disease.

'Your "attitude" to sex, Stacey. Love, if you prefer.'

'No thanks.'

'What does that mean?'

'It means I ain't telling anybody that stuff. Especially not for an assignment.'

'Okay, forget it. How about parents? Are they off-limits?'

Stacey grimaces. 'My parents should be locked away in a cage where they can happily tear each other apart.'

Noah Hennessy walks into the room, carrying his chess board. He sees us chatting and sits in the opposite corner, arranging the pieces carefully, waiting for me to finish with Stacey.

Stacey looks at Noah as if he's an exhibit in a zoo she can't quite identify.

She returns to her parents ripping each other to shreds. 'Pour them wine at night and listen to the battle.' She shivers at the thought.

'I gotta go, Darcy.' She stands and straightens her skirt.

'Definitely anonymous?'

I cross my heart and pretend to spit.

Stacey rolls her eyes again.

She's just spent lunchtime with a boy scout.

'Hey, Noah, what do you think of drugs?'

Noah shrugs. 'Drugs are for people who can't play chess.'

He moves the white pawn and offers me a chair behind the black pieces.

The value of poetry

'All Romantic poets deserve to drown, or die slowly of tuberculosis in a garret.'

I'm standing at the front of class, waiting for universal acclaim from my fellow students.

Audrey smiles.

The others stare blankly.

Marcus Guyotus scribbles hurriedly in his workbook. Perhaps he's going to quote me in an assignment?

Ms Hopkins leans against the side window, frowning. Today's red T-shirt reads 'Corporate Crime' in the Coca-Cola font, complete with the dynamic ribbon. Underneath is the slogan, 'Capitalised profit, socialised debt'.

I add, 'Actually, die quickly, not slowly. If it's too slow, they'll have time to write more tortured verse.'

Audrey chips in, 'That we'll have to study two hundred years after they're dead and buried!'

I volunteered for this.

Earlier, Ms Hopkins offered each student five minutes to rant about whatever we liked. We had thirty minutes to compose a speech on any subject. Shelley and the Romantics came instantly to mind.

Ms Hopkins walks to the front of the classroom and nods for me to take a seat. Audrey gives me the thumbs-up as I walk past. Ms Hopkins leans against her desk.

'Does anyone here like the Romantics?'

No-one raises their hand. We all wriggle uncomfortably in our chairs. Except Marcus, he starts picking his nose.

Ms Hopkins sighs, scanning the room.

'Anyone?'

Marcus begins cleaning his ears.

Ms Hopkins theatrically lowers her head into her hands. I'm not sure if it's genuine anguish or if she's joking. Marcus places his hands in his pockets and wipes his fingers inside.

Ms Hopkins lifts her head. 'Does anyone here like any poetry?'

I'm the only one who raises a hand.

'Yes, Darcy, we know about Shakespeare.' Ms Hopkins smiles. 'Does anyone like music?'

Twelve hands shoot up, Marcus a little behind everyone else.

'And movies?'

Twelve hands stay up.

'Books?'

Marcus begins to lower his hand, then thinks better of it and raises it even higher, in case Ms Hopkins is marking our response.

Ms Hopkins walks over to the bookshelf beside the whiteboard and stares at it. A long, uncomfortable silence. We slowly lower our hands. She reaches up to the middle shelf and selects a volume and walks back to face us, holding the book, cover out. *The Selected Poems of Percy Bysshe Shelley.*

She's going to read a beautiful lilting ballad of lost love, charity and hope, full of words such as 'splendour' and 'majesty'. She'll recite it in a strong voice with perfect rhythm and metre. We'll all be swept along by the narrative.

She is going to prove how wrong I am.

Ms Hopkins opens the book, flipping through the pages. She settles on a poem. I wriggle nervously in my seat, hoping it's not a eight-page elegy. Ms Hopkins clears her throat and walks slowly across the room to the open window where the light is strong. Maybe she needs glasses? She looks at me. '"Ozymandias"; "Ode to the West Wind"; *Prometheus Unbound*; classic poems . . . all as dead as the poet who wrote them?'

Marcus raises his hand. 'Ms, how do you spell Ozymandias?'

'Marcus, this is not for an assignment. We're discussing poetry.'

Marcus puts down his pen and closes his workbook.

Ms Hopkins continues, 'Who wants to hear a poem?'

A collective sigh fills the room.

She adds, 'Think of it as a song without the music.'

Stacey says, 'That's like coffee without the caffeine. Pointless.'

Miranda, 'Yeah, or scotch and soda, without the scotch.'

Marcus, 'Or an Xbox without . . .' His voice trails off, 'the box.'

Ms Hopkins shakes her head, holds the book aloft, her fist curling around the spine. 'A world without poetry . . .' She tugs at her shirt, '. . . is greed and money and avarice.'

In one swift movement, she flings the book out the window. I watch it spin crazily through the air, a mess of pages flapping in vain. It bounces in the dirt, skidding to a halt under a thorny rose bush. A boy from Year Seven walking along the path jumps in fright. He looks up quickly, fearing an airborne assault.

Ms Hopkins calls out, 'Sorry.'

The boy looks under the rose bush to check the carcass.

Ms Hopkins waves at him. 'Leave it there, will you?'

The pages of the book flutter and then die.

We all stand at the window, open-mouthed.

Ms Hopkins walks back to her desk and sits down.

We shuffle our feet like drunk mourners at a wake, not sure who to approach to offer sympathy.

We slowly return to our seats.

Everyone looks at Ms Hopkins, then me, as if I'm to blame?

Marcus raises his hand, tentatively and coughs, to get attention.

'Would you like me to get the book, Ms?'

'No, it's okay, Marcus. It's just a –' She looks at me, 'poetry book.'

What? Am I supposed to feel bad? I didn't force her to throw it out the window. Everyone stares at me.

'I didn't kill the book!'

Marcus rolls his eyes, 'It's not dead – just a little dirty'.

'At least the book finally left the shelves!'

I regret saying it immediately. I've borrowed heaps of books from Ms Hopkins, even Shelley when we were forced to do an assignment on poets.

I mutter, 'I was talking about the Romantics, not real books.'

Ms Hopkins stands and walks to the bookcase. Please, don't toss any more into the garden. She turns to face the class.

'The middle shelf is Shelley, Keats, Wordsworth, Lord Byron.

'Hundreds . . . thousands of poems.

'All unread by Year Eleven.

'What's the difference between these and the Shelley out there under the rose bush?'

I'm tempted to say the Shelley book will rot away to compost and provide nutrition to the plant. It's finally useful!

Ms Hopkins takes a book from the top shelf. Shakespeare. Oh no, not Prince William. *Is this a dagger I see before me.*

She smooths her hand along the cover.

'If no-one reads poetry, what's the point? Why waste paper? Why all that effort, love, time, emotion, only to sit mute and useless, to be so easily neglected. A life ignored, discarded, because no-one cares.'

Noah Hennessy jumps out of his chair.

It scrapes noisily on the floorboards.

My teeth grind.

Noah strides to the door, opens it and says in a tight, low voice, 'Can I be excused?'

Before Ms Hopkins can answer, he closes the door and we hear his footsteps rushing down the verandah to the stairs. We all stand to look out the window. Ms Hopkins walks across the room.

Noah runs to the rose bush, reaches down and picks up the book, shaking the dirt from its pages, checking for damage.

Nothing but a wilted spine.

Noah looks up at us. Marcus is the only person who ducks.

Noah walks slowly back to class.

Ms Hopkins meets him in the hallway. They talk for a few minutes in whispers. Noah gives her the book and she places a hand on his shoulder. They return to the classroom. Noah sits at his desk. He stares at the bookshelf.

Ms Hopkins places the book on her desk and takes a deep breath. 'I'm sorry, Year Eleven. That was much too heavy-handed.'

The bell rings for next period. Ms Hopkins smiles sheepishly. 'I promise no more book-throwing this term. Not even Shelley.'

She looks at me. 'Especially not Shelley.'

I catch up to Noah in the hallway. He's walking quickly to Science in H Block.

'Poetry is it, Noah?'

He shakes his head.

'Come on, Hennessy, out with it? Sucking up to Ms Hopkins isn't your style.'

Noah shifts his schoolbag from one shoulder to the other.

I check my watch.

I've got Physical Education with Mr Thomas on the other side of the school. He doesn't like latecomers. He doesn't like anything much. Except Sport.

'Okay, poetry boy. You and Shelley can drown in verse.'

I wince at my own bad pun.

Noah doesn't bite. He walks into Science class without saying a word. I turn and sprint to the locker room.

Sport

In the change room, I'm overwhelmed by the smell of wet socks and Pine O Cleen. 'Physical Education'. Is that an oxymoron?

The class is already doing laps of the oval, Mr Thomas blasting on his whistle.

'So good of you to join us, Walker. Two laps at half-pace, now.'

Maybe Ms Hopkins is right. At least poetry tries to be beautiful, to enlighten us, to be about something. Sport, on the other hand, is just running around in circles for no apparent reason.

Before setting off, I bend down to tie my shoelaces.

'Walker, I said now!'

'I'm saving the school from a huge insurance claim if I should fall over, sir.'

Mr Thomas laughs cynically. 'I doubt you'll be travelling at a speed fast enough to injure yourself.'

Jogging slowly away, I call back, 'My name is Walker, sir.'

He doesn't get the joke, just blasts on his whistle again as Harris and Miller finish their laps, having barely raised a sweat.

They make a beeline for the football in Mr Thomas's kitbag. Mr Thomas carries a bundle of plastic posts to one end of the oval, digging them into the ground at metre-long intervals. He gets to the end of the line and looks to check if they're straight, walking slowly back to adjust one of the posts.

I've slowed to a shuffle when he looks up and sees me. The whistle blares. I wave to let him know I've heard.

All of the suburb has heard.

When I finish, the rest of the class are sitting on the grass, gasping for breath, while Harris and Miller kick the ball to one another. Miller is wearing a sweatband around his head, possibly to keep his brains from tumbling out. As I slow to a walk, he deliberately kicks the ball at me.

I duck.

He laughs. 'This is Sport, nancy-boy.'

I'd come up with a wisecrack, if I had the breath.

Mr Thomas says, 'Go and pick up the ball, Walker. We'll start our first drill.'

Maybe Shelley was bullied at school and decided to retaliate by writing poetry? He found truth and beauty through words instead of whatever sport they played in his era.

'Mr Thomas, what sport did they play in ancient times?'

Mr Thomas motions for me to pass him the ball. 'This is Sport, Walker. Not History.'

The longer I hold the ball, the less time for Sport.

I suggest, 'Jousting?'

'The ball, Walker.'

'Archery?'

Mr Thomas sneers, 'You lot with weapons!'

Tim says, 'Aussie Rules.'

'What!'

'Aussie Rules. It's been around for ages.'

Marcus suggests, 'Lacrosse.'

Braith scoffs, 'That's not a sport, it's a brand of shirt.'

Mr Thomas yells, 'Walker, the ball!'

I toss it vaguely in his direction.

He has to stoop to catch it and doesn't quite make it.

The ball bounces up and hits him in the knee.

Tim deftly puts his foot under the ball and flicks it into the air, catching it and handing it to Mr Thomas.

'There you go, sir. Can we play footy now?'

To go or not to go

Dad drizzles olive oil into the saucepan and leans down to check the heat is low. He walks to the bench, takes a sip of wine, then starts chopping the garlic.

'Dad, can I get a note for school?'

'You mean a note to miss school.'

'Well, yeah. But not "real" school.'

He laughs to himself, ' "Fantasy" school?'

'No, the excursion. We have to stay out overnight and I won't learn anything.'

'Don't be so negative, Darcy.'

'I reckon half the class isn't going.'

He tips the garlic into the saucepan and starts chopping the onion. Before too long he's sniffling.

'Are you crying because you'll miss me?'

A bit of humour can't hurt.

'Good try, Darcy.' He puts down the knife. 'Here's the deal, you can miss the excursion . . .'

'Great, thanks Dad!'

'I haven't finished, son.' He takes a sip of wine.

'You can miss the excursion if you can convince your mother to write the note.'

'What!'

'The ball's in your court.'

'But you always write the notes.'

He laughs. 'Because you're smart enough to ask me first. Not this time. Try your mum. I'm too much of a pushover.' He wipes his eyes on his sleeve and rinses the knife under the tap. 'Think of it as an exercise in debating.'

'Futility, you mean.'

'Mum, do you think I could get a note for school?'

She looks up from the books, piled high on her study desk. 'No.'

'Can you hear me out before you reach a verdict?'

She puts down her pen and checks her watch. 'Sure. The answer will still be no.'

'What if every judge thought like you?'

'The world would be a more . . .' She removes her glasses, 'just place.'

'What if every judge decided on the outcome before hearing the argument. Your argument.'

'This is not a courtroom, Darcy. Even if you look guilty.'

She can barely contain a smile.

'It's the excursion, Mum. Camping out overnight. With snakes and . . .' I can't think of any other dangerous animals, 'Wombats and koalas.'

'You know as well as I do, Darcy, there's no good reason I should write you a note.'

'I can think of a few bad reasons.'

'And why are you asking me? You always ask . . . Oh, I see, you've already asked David. And he's said "no" as well.'

'But he was crying when he said it.'

A look of concern knots her brow. 'Your father was crying?'

'Maybe he felt guilty for not writing a note.'

'Darcy?'

'Possibly there were onions involved.'

Mum picks up her glasses. 'I'm working on a very serious case at present, Darcy.'

'Does it involve a teenager divorcing his parents?'

'You'll have a great time, believe me.' As I turn to leave, she laughs. 'Watch out for the koalas, son.'

The school excursion

Kayaking, for six hours down the Kangaroo River. The forecast is for sunshine, a gentle breeze and mass student drownings. Mr Jackson and Ms Pine, our year-level teachers, talk at length about team-building exercises and learning to trust each other, to extend ourselves.

Silly bastards.

Marcus has already pulled out, handing a note to Mr Jackson.

His mother doesn't practise law.

He slinks off to the library for two days of pawing through astronomy books while the rest of us load our packs onto the bus.

I've never been in a kayak before.

None of us have.

Ms Pine says it's like a canoe only different. She's like a teacher, only different.

Tim and Braith and a few of their mates have boarded the bus early and seized the back row. They put their feet up on the seats in front, daring anyone to come near.

I'd rather stick my head in a cow pat.

I bag a spot midway down, beside the window, and quietly pray for Audrey to sit beside me.

Noah plonks himself down.

He wriggles uncomfortably for a moment and smiles awkwardly at me. He has forgiven me my slight on poets.

Audrey sits two seats in front. Her hair is pulled back in a tight bun with a chopstick holding it in place. I'd like to take the stick out, watch her heavy hair fall free and then poke Noah in the eye with the chopstick.

Noah reaches into the bag at his feet and takes out his chess board. He opens it between us. We still haven't spoken.

'You want a game, do you, Noah?'

He arranges the pieces, then moves the pawn forward. 'It might be a fun trip.'

If he asks me to share the kayak with him, I'll throw his chess set out the window.

'Why don't we share a kayak, Darcy?'

I lean in close, in case anybody else hears. 'Jackson says everyone has to share with a girl.'

Noah looks a little confused. 'Even the girls?'

'What?'

He starts counting everyone on the bus, pointing at each person, mouthing the numbers. His eyebrows meet in the middle like two caterpillars doing battle, bushy arms and legs flailing.

He says, 'There are fourteen girls and fourteen boys.'

'That's right, Noah.'

'So, for everyone to share with a girl . . .' he does the equation in his head, 'there would have to be twenty-eight girls and fourteen boys.'

What in hell is he talking about?

'It's mathematically impossible with our current numbers.'

We are five minutes into the school camp and already I'm lost. The bus is only now turning onto the main south road.

The driver leans forward and turns on the radio. If I'm not mistaken that crooning voice belongs to

Frank Sinatra. Braith farts loudly from the rear – pardon the pun – of the bus. The driver sings along with Frankie.

Noah says, 'Oh! I get it. You mean every *boy* shares with a girl!'

A little old lady with a walker waits at the intersection. She leans heavily on her support, not sure if she should cross the street or wait until she gets her breath back.

'You said every *one* shares with a girl. That's what I couldn't understand.'

'Noah, each girl will share a boat with a boy. Understand!'

'A kayak.'

'What?'

'A kayak. Mr Jackson said not to call them boats.'

'Mr Jackson says not to call him Jacko the Wacko, but everyone does.'

Noah smiles conspiratorially, as though we're smoking a joint at the back of the bus.

Which reminds me. Tim and Braith. Chances are . . .

Tim has his head half out the window. He's spitting on the passing roof of a Mercedes Sports. Braith is laughing and slapping him on the back. Tim pulls his head back in just as a semi-trailer roars past the bus.

There's no weed in sight. If they've brought any, it's packed deep in Tim's luggage for later tonight.

Braith sees me watching.

He points his finger at me, like he's holding a gun. He fires. Then he blows the barrel. He stands and acts like he's tucking it back into his holster.

Braith has seen too many cowboy movies.

He'd be well suited to the black hat role.

Noah whispers, 'Why is Braith shooting you with his finger?'

'Because his gun's in the backpack.'

Noah laughs, the chessboard flies off his lap, the pieces scatter across the floor. He clutches at the board before it lands.

He looks at me like he's been shot.

By Braith's finger?

Then he starts picking up each of the chess pieces, scrambling around on the floor. I stand up to help.

Every time the bus turns a corner, a piece rolls away from us, under a seat.

We're both on our knees, stretching under the seats.

No-one else moves.

Noah crawls under the seat occupied by Jessica Wells and Rosa Paccula.

Rosa yells, 'Do you mind?'

Noah quickly backs out, turning to me.

I point underneath the seat and say, 'It's the chess pieces. We've dropped them.'

Jessica sneers at me like I'm a complete nerd.

'Whatcha want them for?' she says.

Noah answers, 'To play chess!'

Bugger this. I quickly duck down and reach between her feet, grabbing the piece.

She screams.

Mr Jackson calls out, 'What's happening back there?'

Noah says, 'We've lost the pawn, sir.'

Oh dear!

Braith and Tim bellow with laughter.

'Who's got porn!'

Noah blushes bright red.

Mr Jackson walks slowly down the aisle on the lookout for dirty magazines.

Braith calls out, 'Come on, Noah, show us your porn.'

Each time he says the word 'porn' every boy in the back row starts laughing. Tim Harris is making obscene gestures to the rest of the bus, while Mr Jackson looks at Noah and demands an answer.

I step in front of Noah and hold up the rook. 'Noah dropped his chess set, sir.'

Tim calls out, 'We've got spare porn down the back, if anyone's interested.'

Cue ten boys laughing.

'Yeah, girls, live porn.'

Mr Jackson pretends not to hear.

He tells Noah to be more careful next time.

Jacko the Wimpo returns to his seat.

Tim and Braith keep laughing as the bus stops at a traffic light.

Tim points out the window. 'Look, fellas, it's the red-light district.'

This is, even by Harris standards, a pathetic joke.

'You should hop out and visit your mum, Tim.'

Did I really say that?

All the boys laugh, instinctively, then stop when they see Tim's face. It's red, and mean, and ugly.

And heading my way.

He swears as he runs down the aisle.

Not even Jackson can ignore this.

Noah dives across the seat to get out of Tim's way. There's nowhere for me to go. Harris jumps and lunges for my neck. I quickly raise my arms to deflect the blow. The force of his leap knocks me backwards against the seat, the air crushed from my lungs. Harris lands on top of me.

Rosa screams.

The bus driver brakes quickly, not sure if the scream he's heard came from inside or out. Everyone grips onto their seat to steady themselves, except me and Tim. We tumble onto the floor. Tim tries to punch me in the stomach but I grip both his arms tightly, lessening the blows.

We're in a macabre dance. Tim leads, I hang on for dear life.

I'm gasping for breath as Tim tries to pummel me. Haven't we been through this before? Tim's only had the bandage off for a few days. His wrist seems to be working fine though. It's wrapped around my neck. And squeezing.

Mr Jackson stands over both of us, shouting, 'Harris, let him go!'

Tim does a excellent impression of a deaf mute.

I remember watching a nature program with Dad. We both squirmed on the lounge as a giant boa constrictor squeezed the life out of a baby lamb. The lamb kept trying to bleat but no sound came.

Tim tightens his grip, his bicep bulging against my throat.

'Harris, I'll count to ten.'

Ten! Make it five. Or three! I'm having trouble bleating.

Mr Jackson grabs Tim by the collar and tries to haul him off me. Ms Pine gets a hand in as well. They both pull together.

The ripping sound is Tim's shirt, not my throat.

Ms Pine staggers back holding a piece of cloth.

Mr Jackson drags Harris off.

I scurry backwards like a frightened crab.

I'd get up if I had my breath back. Maybe in a little while. Say, thirty minutes?

Mr Jackson nods to the driver to start again and tells everyone to sit down. I'm glad no-one has asked me to talk. My throat is on fire.

Noah carefully packs all his pieces back into the set.

He's trying not to look in my direction, like a motorist late for an appointment passing a road accident.

I wouldn't mind a nice quiet game of chess right now.

Maybe a cup of tea and a good lie-down as well.

Everyone knows Tim's mum left home last year and hasn't been seen since. Rumour is she packed the clapped-out station wagon one morning before the family woke and drove off, leaving a note on the kitchen table. The neighbours said when Tim's dad got home from shiftwork, he threw all her belongings in the garden and lit a huge bonfire.

Soon after, I walked past their place.

Tim was spreading sand over the scorched grass.

He saw me passing and sneered.

Ms Pine looks from Tim to me to Mr Jackson.

She says, 'We've got twenty-four hours together, boys.

'Let's try a little harder, shall we?'

Tim grunts.

Mr Jackson adds, 'I don't want to have to write a report to Mrs Archer. Let's call it over-exuberance.'

Tim grunts again.

I extend my hand. 'Sorry, Tim.'

We shake and Tim walks to the rear of the bus. Mr Jackson looks at Ms Pine, shrugs his shoulders and returns to his seat. Ms Pine pats my shoulder and follows him.

Plonking myself down next to Noah, I look out the window for a very long time. Noah keeps fidgeting in his seat wanting to say something.

But he thinks better of it.

In the valley, in the bus

The bus rattles down the mountain, the road shaded by stands of ghost gums.

In the distance, cows graze in the green valley and a ramshackle windmill spins crookedly. On the side of a barn, a sign reads, 'Chickens for sale. Dead or alive'.

You can buy a pet for the children – or dinner.

As the road levels, a row of trees shields the river twisting through the valley.

Half the students are asleep, the other half are listening to iPods. Audrey sits a few rows in front staring out the window.

I'm embarrassed about the fight with Tim, for letting my big mouth get the better of me. It was a cheap shot about his mum.

Audrey stands and walks down the aisle to my seat. She leans in to Noah and says, 'Why don't you take my seat? Then you can stretch out.'

It's probably the closest he's been to a female since childbirth.

He looks quickly at me and tightens his grip on the chess board.

'Where . . . where will you sit?'

'I'll sit with Darcy. I want to ask him about English homework.'

I touch his arm. 'It's okay, Noah. We'll have a game later tonight. Beside the campfire.'

Visions of plastic chess pieces melting in the flames.

Noah stands slowly and nervously moves past Audrey, worried about parts of his body touching parts of her body.

I have a similar fear, Noah.

Audrey sits beside me. 'I came to protect you from evil Tim.'

'Me and Noah could handle Tim and Braith. No worries.'

Audrey whispers, 'Yeah, you'd bore them to death with chess.'

Can we press the pause button for a moment?

Everyone has a screensaver image they like to

look at, right: an expanse of ocean, a snow-capped mountain, trees swaying in the breeze, a picture of our closest friend. We can spend hours gazing wistfully, drifting, blissfully lost. It's meditation for people who can't sit cross-legged in the backyard and hum.

My parents would call it soul quality time.

What I'm trying to say is looking at Audrey does it for me.

No, it's not frantic rumblings of erections and naked bodies wrapped together, if that's what you're thinking. It's almost – cue *Twilight Zone* music – mystical.

Okay?

Pure and simple.

No sleaze.

Just admiration.

Audrey clicks her fingers, quietly.

'Are you still with me, Darcy?'

'Sorry, I was thinking of meditation. We should try it together sometime. You can show me how.'

'It's meant to be done alone, in a quiet place, like my backyard.' She raises one eyebrow. 'With no-one watching.'

The bus steadily climbs a hill, the driver wrestling with the gearstick.

The grating is putting my teeth on edge.

Mr Jackson is telling Ms Pine all about the finer points of fibreglass kayaks versus plastic. Jessica and Rosa are pointing and laughing at pictures in a glossy magazine, their squeals designed to attract the attention of the boys slouching in the back row.

'Audrey, I like to sit on my roof and look at the . . . cliffs.'

Her eyebrow arches, just that little bit higher.

I wriggle uncomfortably in my seat. 'Okay. I admit it! I'll never do it again. Ever!'

Mr Jackson shows Ms Pine the correct way to wear a life jacket. He struggles with the plastic buckle meant to fit snugly around his waist.

It doesn't quite reach.

Mr Jackson's face turns red.

'I knew you were there, Darcy.'

This is more uncomfortable than playing chess with Noah.

Audrey leans forward and grips the metal bar on the seat in front. 'It's okay. I didn't really think you were perving.'

In the clear light of day, what else was it!

I swallow hard.

'I tried meditating once, on the roof.'

'Did it work?'

'I kept falling asleep. My head drooping forward until I'd wake and not know where I was.'

'I've done that. Sometimes, when I'm really blissed out, I dribble.'

She looks quickly behind, hoping Jessica and Rosa haven't heard.

They're still off with Paris or Lindsay in skank heaven.

'The other day, when I caught you perving – I mean, looking at the cliffs – did you duck?'

'Nah. It was a trick of the light. Why would I duck?'

'Darcy?'

I raise both hands, in surrender.

'Guilty. And I'll never do it again. I promise.'

The campground

Twenty-eight students stand around a stack of dry twigs and rolled up newspaper. Mr Jackson and Ms Pine talk in hushed tones. Surely, someone has brought some matches. It'll be dark in less than an hour. A crow drolls from the highest branch.

'I could get it going, if ya want?'

It's the second time Tim has spoken since we arrived at the campsite.

The first time was when he stepped off the bus, looked around at the featureless scrub and said 'shit' in a very loud voice.

Mr Jackson grimaced. 'That'll be enough, Tim. It's not so bad.'

Stacey added, 'It's a pile of weeds, sir. We can't sleep here.'

The sign read 'Roberts Campground'. Fifty square metres of patchy grass, a few fallen logs rotting along one side, the river on the other and a track leading off into the bush.

Jessica was the first to mention the key word.

''Toilets?'

Mr Jackson walked to the pile of gear and picked up a shovel. He held it out to Jessica. She backed away.

He smiled and pointed at her magazine.

'And that'll come in handy too.'

Mr Jackson claps his hands.

'Okay, anyone have a match?'

Quick as a flash, Braith replies, 'Sure, my arse and Darcy's face.'

'Yes, sir, it's where Braith keeps his brain.'

Braith spits and threatens to shoot me with his finger again.

Mr Jackson elaborately removes a box of matches from his jacket pocket.

'I wondered how many of you came prepared.'

Tim repeats, 'I could get it going, if ya want.'

He seems unduly interested in burning things.

Mr Jackson tosses him the matchbox.

'Okay, Tim has the fire. The rest of you start unpacking your gear. You can sleep anywhere within ten metres of the fire. Not too close.

'The kayaks will be arriving early tomorrow.'

Ms Pine adds, 'There'll be no sharing of sleeping bags. You understand?'

We all scatter, looking for the softest patch of grass among the weeds.

I carry my sleeping bag towards the river, Noah close behind.

I turn left, then right, circle back on myself. Noah follows, like a lost puppy.

Audrey is close to the logs on the far side of the camp. It would be a little obvious to walk straight across and plonk myself down beside her.

As obvious as Noah standing beside me.

'This looks good here, Darcy?'

'Yeah, Noah. It's fine.'

He spreads his sleeping bag out, doing the zip up full.

He grins sheepishly. 'In case anything climbs inside when I'm at the fire.'

'What, like Stacey Scott?'

Noah shivers at the thought, glancing across to Stacey and Miranda sitting on their bags, suspiciously close to Braith and the rest of the blokes.

It's going to be a long night of dirty jokes, giggling and Mr Jackson shouting for everyone to go to sleep.

'I wish I'd brought my pillow.' Noah says.

Claire Rusina has arranged her sleeping bag next to Audrey. No chance of me creeping over there later tonight. Not that I've got enough guts anyway.

It's me and Noah.

He places the chessboard on his bag.

'We can have a game before bed, Darcy. I would have won last time, I reckon.'

He looks furtively at Tim.

Tim is busy lighting another match and swearing. Mr Jackson stands beside him.

'It needs more paper, Tim.'

Tim coughs, overwhelmed by smoke.

It hasn't rained in days but the kindling is damp with dew. Somewhere high in the forest, a wattlebird cackles. Everyone carries their dinner boxes towards the wood stack, waiting for Tim, or Mr Jackson.

The sound of snoring comes from the bus.

Mr Carney, the bus driver, is already asleep on the back seat. It's his job to pick us up at the other end of the river.

Braith suggests, 'We can drain the fuel tank on the bus, pour it on and we'll have a blaze going in no time.'

Ms Pine rolls her eyes. 'And a bushfire half-way to town.'

Braith laughs. 'No worries. We'll jump in the river.'

The smoke is getting worse.

Noah says, 'We could all try blowing on it.'

Everyone looks at Noah. To give them credit, no-one speaks.

As if on cue, a light breeze starts the paper burning.

The twigs crackle as the fire takes hold.

Tim stands and bows as a few people clap.

We all crowd around the growing flames.

Everyone unwraps the sandwiches. White bread and cheese.

Tim groans. 'How can we eat this shit?'

Mr Jackson looks hurt. 'The canteen ladies prepared these especially for us, Tim.'

'Why don't we drive back to McDonald's?' Jessica steps from one foot to the other, 'For food and toilets.'

Mr Jackson ignores her and takes a huge bite of his sandwich, pretending it tastes good.

Braith picks up a long twig and stabs his sandwich. He swaggers to the fire and holds it over the flames. 'Toasted cheese sanga!'

The twig breaks and the sandwich falls into the fire.

Braith reaches for a packet of corn chips and swears.

After dinner, I casually saunter over to stand near Audrey. Claire is rubbing her hands and talking non-stop. Audrey doesn't notice me beside her. Above the crackle and spit of the flaming logs, I hear Claire's monologue –

'He's got his own car and he lives with his brother, in a flat near the beach. At first, the smell of dead meat put me off, but he'd scrub his hands with ti-tree oil.

Isn't that sweet? I never met a butcher before. I kept thinking of blood and gristle under his fingernails, uggghhh! Anyway, he's better than any boy at school.'

As she says this, I can't help but cough.

I blame the smoke.

Audrey notices me.

'Hey, Darcy. Claire and me were talking about boys. Join in.'

'What would I know about boys? I mean, apart from myself.'

That didn't come out quite right. I do not have masturbatory fantasies!

'Claire was telling me about her new boyfriend. A butcher.'

'Nice.'

Claire doesn't like my tone.

'Well, at least he's got a job. And he's much older than you!'

'And you know, he'll always be older than me. Even when I'm eighty.'

'What's that supposed to mean?'

Noah calls from the other side of the fire, 'Hey Darcy, look what I've got!'

He waves a packet of marshmallows.

Claire smirks, 'Better go eat lollies with your pal, Walker.'

Audrey doesn't meet my eyes.

I contemplate shoving a whole bag of marshmallows down Claire's throat.

Noah suggests we toast them on the fire.

Soggy cheese sandwiches and burnt marshmallows. The night couldn't get much better.

I walk to my sleeping bag and climb in, pulling the flap over my head.

It's warm and quiet inside.

Noah opens the chessboard.

Tim calls, 'Still got ya porn, Noah?'

Giggles from the girls, loud laughter from Tim and Braith.

Braith says, 'You can learn a lot from magazines, Hennessy.'

I dearly want to yell, 'Only if you can read!'

Tim Harris farts.

It's amazing how far noise travels in the dark.

Mr Jackson calls out, 'Time for bed everyone, we've got a big day tomorrow.'

Everyone climbs into their sleeping bags. Tim, Braith and a few girls have arranged their bags close to the edge of the campground, where the firelight barely reaches.

An owl hoots from the trees across the river and one of the girls giggles again. Above us, a plane drones at ten thousand metres. Claire says to no-one in particular, 'I should have brought a pillow.'

Braith answers. 'You can rest your head on my stomach, if ya want.'

'In your dreams, Miller.'

Mr Jackson makes a sound like a punctured gas cylinder. 'SSSSSHHHHHH!'

It's quiet for all of five minutes when I hear the sound of shuffling and urgent whispers. Harris has made a play to climb in with Stacey. I peek out from under my hood and see a figure crawling back to his bag.

Tough luck, Tim.

A sound of a bag being zipped up is followed by a fart and another burst of laughing, this time only from the boys.

Noah coughs. 'Pssst.'

I pretend to be asleep.

'Psssst!'

I fake snoring, badly.

'Darcy?'

'Go to sleep, Noah.'

'I want to show you something.'

Please don't let Tim hear that.

'Tomorrow, for God's sake.'

Noah unzips his bag and pulls something out from underneath. It looks like . . .

'Bloody hell!'

'It's not real, Darcy.'

He holds up a long plastic snake. In the darkness, it looks suspiciously menacing and live.

'We can throw it over there and see what happens.'

'It's a little childish, Noah.'

'What, more juvenile than farting and porn?'

'Okay, do what you like. Just don't involve me.'

Noah grins insanely and launches the snake on its way with all his strength.

'Shit! Shit!'

Tim jumps up, still in his bag, and staggers across the campground. He's madly trying to unzip the bag and run at the same time. He stumbles and falls, rolling in the dirt.

'It's a monster!'

Jessica Wells sees the snake coiled in the grass and quickly pulls the bag over her head, rolling herself in a tight little ball. Claire closes her eyes and screams. Both are obviously devotees of the 'what we can't see, can't hurt us' brigade.

Tim frees his hands from the sleeping bag and frantically rubs his hair as if the poison is seeping into his brain.

'It's a death adder! It landed on my head.'

He unzips his bag and scrambles out, grabs a log from the fire and holds it in front of him, searching for the snake. He looks like a berserk warrior wearing Mickey Mouse boxer shorts.

Tim lurches towards the girls, the log crackling and spitting sparks. 'I'm gunna kill it!'

Mr Jackson approaches, holding up both hands. 'Calm down, Tim. It's gone now. All that noise would scare anything away.'

Tim points to something beside Claire and runs towards it. Claire opens her eyes and sees Tim marauding, flaming log ready to strike. She screams once, then faints, dropping in her sleeping bag like a sack of sad potatoes. Ms Pine rushes towards her and lifts her head, clearing the airways.

It's a faint, not a fit!

Tim stands over the plastic monster. 'You bastard!'

He beats it senseless with his burning log, hitting the snake so hard it bounces.

It's fighting back!

The plastic snake is fighting back!

Tim belts it again and again, sparks hiss and fly and the snake is melting. I can smell the putrid scent of blistering plastic.

Noah yells, 'It's a toy!'

Everyone stops moving. Even Ms Pine leaves Claire's tongue alone and looks toward the snake. Tim holds the log close to the snake's head and sees the colours, all bright and shiny and melty and very, very unlifelike. Or whatever the word is that means plastic.

Claire stirs briefly beside Ms Pine and looks at the snake. She's about to scream again so Ms Pine puts her hand over Claire's mouth. 'It's a toy, Claire. Nothing to worry about.'

Claire removes Ms Pine's hand from her mouth, as any self-respecting teenage girl would do, gets out of her sleeping bag and walks quickly into the bushes.

To go to the toilet, I suspect.

Or to find a real snake to throw back at Noah.

And where is Noah?

He's quietly returned to his sleeping bag, climbed inside and zipped it up.

I hope he doesn't have a zoo of plastic animals hiding in there. A goanna, a crocodile, a spider – all ready to launch across the campground at unsuspecting sleepers in the night.

Our nerves couldn't stand it.

Ms Pine stands. 'Everyone back to bed. We'll discuss this tomorrow.'

Tim hurls the log as far as he can throw it into the river. Sparks flicker over the blazing trail and I picture catastrophic bushfires broadcast on the evening news for the next week. Smoke-affected teenagers rescued by helicopters with one nerdy kid holding what looks suspiciously like a melted chess set, Mr Jackson valiantly trying to explain how it all started.

A plastic snake, a berserk warrior.

Tim swears loudly and repeatedly as he walks back to his sleeping bag.

He looks across at me.

I try to look innocent.

I AM INNOCENT!

Tim doesn't seem to think so. He says 'shit' once more before climbing back into his bag. Mr Jackson winces at the language, then buries the plastic snake in a shallow grave, muttering darkly about toxic fumes and bad language.

Noah

Noah wakes impulsively early, pokes his head out of the sleeping bag and whispers, 'Psst, Darcy. You want to watch the sunrise?'

Short answer?

'Piss off!'

Long answer?

'Piss off, Noah!'

Noah shuffles around in his bag until I begin to get a little suspicious of what he's doing. I hope no-one wakes and hears him.

Can't he do it somewhere discreet?

Like Africa, or the wild jungle of his bedroom.

Noah rolls over and grunts, banging his head on his boots beside the sleeping bag. He says 'damn' quietly and then unzips the bag and quickly climbs out, rubbing his hands with the cold. He's fully dressed.

So that's what he was doing in the bag. Thank God and the Cat Empire.

He reaches across for his boots and slips them on.

He walks down to the river and sits beside the bank.

The mist rises from the water and a long-legged bird on the opposite bank searches for food. The dull orange glow of the sun peeks over the hill. It's like a romantic early Australian painting of the virgin bush. If only the virgin Noah wasn't sitting in the foreground.

The sound of snoring comes from beyond the fire. There's no chance of more sleep, so I try to get dressed undercover.

No wonder Noah did all that grunting.

After ten minutes of wrestling with jeans, shirt, sweater and socks that really should visit a laundry immediately, I climb out of the bag and walk down to the river.

The virgin bushman has the only log dry enough to sit on. I deposit myself a suitable distance away, hoping he'll let me quietly enjoy the sunrise.

'I slept fine, Darcy. Just like in a real bed.'

'Ugghh.'

'That was pretty funny last night. Tim sure looked stupid. And scared.'

Not half as scared as you'll be when he tries to get even later on, Noah.

I look at the dreaming mist, the glassy river, the soft light, a whisper of cloud. Which reminds me.

'So what is it with you and poetry, Noah?'

He looks at me, confused.

'Rescuing dead books from rose bushes. Remember?'

'Nothing.'

'Come on, Noah. Fess up.'

He glances back at the sleeping camp.

'Can I tell you a secret?'

'Not if it involves plastic snakes and chess.'

Noah's voice is quiet. 'My dad came home from work on Monday last week. First thing he does is switch on the television for his favourite quiz show. He tries to beat the contestant, you know. He can't hear the correct answer over his own voice. He thinks he's right, even when he's wrong. Sometimes I sit with him and we both yell at the screen.'

'That's not much of a secret, Noah.'

'We were watching the show and Dad starts stammering, trying to get the words out, only nothing comes, just a squawk, like a sick bird. A little bit of dribble leaks from his mouth, not foamy or anything, just dribble. He still can't get the word out. Mum looks at me as if I know what to do? Dad reaches up to wipe his mouth and his arm starts jerking and waving uncontrollably in front of his face, like he's conducting an orchestra.'

Noah shakes his head. 'Mum reaches out to hold his arm. His eyes lose focus, his jaw goes slack, his head tips forward, his body slumps. Mum screams, as if the noise can stop him falling. And do you know what I do? Come on, guess?'

I don't know what to say.

'Nothing. Dad is fading away in front of me.'

His voice is tense. 'Mum shouts my name and I snap out of it and call an ambulance.'

Noah sighs and closes his eyes, remembering.

A gaggle of ducks fly in formation down the river, their necks craning forward.

'They took ten minutes to arrive. Me and Mum sat beside Dad, each holding a hand. Mum kept saying "You'll be okay, dear," but I don't think he could hear.

'When they wheeled him outside to the ambulance, all of the neighbours were standing around. The ambulance driver came up to me and said he'd be okay.

'I wonder how many times she says that each day?

'Mum jumped in the back with Dad and they drove off.'

Across the water, the long-legged bird digs in the mud. There are tears in Noah's eyes.

'He's still in hospital. He can't talk. One side of his face is slack.

'Mum holds a glass with a straw. He sucks as hard as he can and the water dribbles out. Me and Mum sit either side of his bed, looking at him.

'He closes his eyes, probably bored with us.'

Noah shakes his head.

'We can't ask him questions because he can't answer, can he? He can't hold a pen to write anything. Mum gets me to tell him about school.

'Bloody hell. I never told him when he was well. Why would he want to hear that stuff now?'

Noah looks down at his shoe.

A lady bug walks slowly along the laces. He reaches down and flicks it away.

The bug lands on a rock and keeps walking.

'I tell him school is good. What else can I do? Dad stares across the room at the bloke in the opposite bed. The man has a tube attached to his arm and it goes up to a machine on one of those stands with a bag of fluid. They're feeding him through the tube. The machine beside his bed makes a humming noise. Dad stares at this man. And I stare at Dad.'

Noah takes a deep breath –

'He has dark bristles on his chin, flecked with grey. But the hair doesn't grow evenly. There are bits where it's shaded and full and other bits, just below the ear, where it looks smooth. His face can't even grow a beard properly any more. Dad used to shave every day for work. Mum asked the nurse and she said they shave patients once a week.'

Noah rubs his own chin, thinking aloud.

'I tell Mum I'll shave him if she doesn't want to. I can do it. I look at the folds of his skin, imagining how I'm going to do it. I don't even know if he uses an electric shaver or a razor. I hope it's electric. I whisper in his ear, "I'll be careful, Dad. Don't worry."'

Noah sighs. 'He smiles, even though his mouth stays limp and crooked. His eyes flicker. Just enough to tell me that it's okay, me shaving him.'

Noah reaches down for a small round pebble. He tosses it as high as he can and it lands in the middle of the river, barely disturbing the smooth surface.

'And that's what I'm going to do, Darcy. Shave my dad until he comes back to us. A whole person again.'

I want to reach across and give Noah a manly hug, to let him know there's someone who cares, to reassure him his dad will pull through, but I hear sounds of waking schoolboys coming from the campsite.

'But why get the poetry book, Noah? What's that got to do ...'

'Ms Hopkins said something about a life discarded and I reacted. I don't give a shit about poetry.'

Noah gets up without looking at me and walks back to the campfire.

****

The smell of sausages and bacon drifts from the barbecue Mr Jackson has set up beside the bus. Should naked flames, gas bottles and petrol tanks be in close proximity? Bellbirds, hidden in the high branches, call to each other to come and watch the explosion. We stand in line, each of us holding a single slice of white bread. As we reach the barbecue, Mr Jackson says 'Bacon or sausage'. Audrey, Stacey and Miranda, the vegetarians, choose tomato sauce smeared over their slice of bread, laden with extra onions. Onions cooked in bacon fat. Tim asks for bacon *and* sausage. Mr Jackson doesn't have the energy to say no.

Noah sits on his sleeping bag, chewing slowly, staring towards the river. Audrey stands beside the fire, alone. I know where I want to go, but I'm not totally heartless. And besides, Claire has just walked over to Audrey for Part Two of *Me and the pork chop story*. Maybe her butcher provided today's breakfast?

Noah finishes his white bread breakfast.

'Do you think Jacko will give us seconds?'

'Noah, have you seen how much dead animal is on the barbie?'

Noah walks to the bus. He turns and says, 'You want extra, buddy?'

Buddy!

Buddy!!

I shake my head, quickly glancing at Tim. He's stuffed a whole slice of bread and two sausages into his mouth. He wants to say something, I'm sure, but it's taking him too long to swallow all that food. I have a sudden vision of prehistoric cavemen sitting around the campfire, gorging on an enormous leg of meat, blood dripping at their feet as a woolly mammoth lumbers towards them from out of the jungle. The last thing Caveman One (let's call him Tim) says to his hairy friend is, 'Ummm, tasty.'

And then both of them get squashed flat. Pancakes.

A-rowing we will go . . .

'Mr Jackson, I have a suggestion.'
'Not now, Darcy.'

He's counting the canoes, again.

'There's fifteen, sir. Two people per canoe.'

'Kayaks! They're kayaks, not canoes. How many times have I said that.'

Mr Jackson has been a little testy since Ms Pine suggested they move the barbecue away from the bus. He sulked until the kayaks arrived. They were unloaded by two hairy outdoor types in waterproof jackets and rayon trousers. They dumped them by the

river, counted the paddles, the lifejackets, the canoes
– sorry, kayaks – got Mr Jackson to sign a form and
told us they'd meet us at the dam in six hours. The
one with the beard and the rasta hair jumped back
into the truck and smiled at us. He stuck his head out
the window and said, 'Easy'.

They drove away in a haze of dust.

Easy.

'I have a suggestion, sir. About sharing the kayaks.'

'Yes, yes, Darcy, you can go with Noah.'

He turns to the group,

'Come on everybody, pair up. Life jackets on.'

He fiddles with the buckle to his jacket, trying to
tighten it.

'Boy–girl, sir. That's what we should do.'

He's not listening, so involved in the simple
difficulties of putting on a life jacket. Everyone is
pairing up, dragging the kayaks into the shallows
and tumbling aboard. Noah walks among the kayaks,
trying to decide which one is the most seaworthy.
Riverworthy?

'Hey Darcy, let's get the blue one.'

'Mr Jackson!' I almost shout his name. He looks
up quickly as if I've fallen into the river and he may
have to dive in, life jacket or not.

'Sir. Why don't we go boy–girl in the kayaks?'

Tim and Braith are already sitting in a green kayak, life jackets untied, paddles pushing away from the bank. Mr Jackson sees them and calls out, 'Hold on, you two. It's not a race.'

Which is exactly what Tim and Braith think it is as they paddle out to mid-stream.

Mr Jackson grabs the bow of the nearest kayak and calls to Ms Pine.

He looks at me and says, 'Find somebody will you, Walker.'

Claire Rusina is standing on the sand calling to Audrey. Audrey looks at me and shrugs as if to say, 'What can I do?'

My ideal answer is 'hit Noah and Claire with a paddle!'

Audrey and Claire push off.

Noah pulls the kayak into the water,

'Hurry up, Darcy. We don't want to be left behind.'

Oh yes we do, Noah.

The first splash of water hits me in the face.

Noah paddles like an ironman high on caffeine.

Except he keeps lifting the paddle out of the water at the wrong time. He doesn't stroke so much as flap.

Or flail.

Or flounder.

There's another f-word I'd like to use, but I'm too busy wiping drops of water from my face.

'Just stroke, you goose!'

He turns around, a hurt look on his face.

'No need for names, Darcy. It's my first time.'

He's telling me something I don't already know?

'Watch me, Noah.'

I dip the paddle in the water and sweep it slowly alongside the boat. Then I do it on the opposite side.

'Slow and long, okay, Noah. Don't splash.'

He nods and digs his paddle so far into the water the kayak tips alarmingly to one side. I quickly grab the cockpit, expecting to roll, leaning desperately the other way so the kayak rights itself. We rock to and fro for a few seconds like drunken sailors on a barstool.

Noah yells, 'Sorry,' and takes a deep breath.

This time he executes a beautiful flowing stroke.

Except he doesn't put the paddle into the water. The whoosh of murderous paddle fans my skull.

'Almost got you!'

I'm glad someone thinks this is funny.

After five minutes of crisscrossing the river trying to head in a straight line, we achieve some mad pattern to our stroke work. Noah splashes and flails as I chart a course heading downstream. We don't bother keeping up with most of the group, floating quietly along a few metres behind Stacey and Miranda. While Miranda strains, Stacey rests the paddle across the kayak, lies back in the seat and lets her hands drift along in the water.

I wonder if there are bass in the river. Could they mistake Stacey's fingers for fingerlings? One bite should be enough.

Actually, it's not a bad idea. The simple way to get out of camp. All you lose is the tip of a finger.

A squadron of insects skim the river surface, poking tongues at the trout lurking below. We glide over weeds, submerged logs, the water stained rust brown.

Noah whistles a tune. The back of his head resembles an inverted triangle. Thin neck, pinned-back ears, expanding to an over-sized brain. The stringy red hair looks like it's never seen a comb, a brush, or shampoo.

Did Shakespeare ever go shopping for shampoo in the Elizabethan supermarket, reading the label on the bottle, trying to decide whether it offered his hair a better chance than plain soap? Did he use that piercing intellect to study the ingredients label and make a conscious choice? And did Mrs Shakespeare make her husband take out the rubbish every Wednesday night? He's in the book-lined study, deep into the love scene of *A Midsummer Night's Dream* as his wife calls from the kitchen.

William mutters, 'The course of true love never did run smooth.'

And did he have to take the dog for a walk in the park, looking the other way when it did its business? What sort of dog would Shakespeare own? A daschund. A German shepherd. Certainly not a greyhound. Genius and greyhounds don't go together.

Much like Noah and kayaks.

Noah turns to me, grinning. 'Hey Darcy. I feel just like Huckleberry Finn!'

We round the bend. Most of the group are pulling their kayaks onto a sandy beach. Tim and Braith take off their shirts and dive into the river, splashing the girls, trying to coax them into a swim. Tim's laughter cackles over the constant splashing of Noah's paddling.

I recline in my seat.

Noah paddles even harder.

'Relax, Noah.'

He turns and whispers, 'I don't want to be last.'

He flicks his head towards Stacey and Miranda. We're the only two kayaks left in the river.

Noah says, 'Come on, buddy.'

A splash of water hits me in the face. Noah is doing this with or without me.

He's so obvious, even Miranda notices. She starts paddling faster, urging Stacey to help. Stacey grips hard and joins in. They paddle like crazy windmills in a hurricane.

Noah grins. 'We can do it, Darcy!'

He digs the paddle in deep and swishes.

Too deep.

130

The kayak tips awkwardly. I'm leaning too far back to help. Noah panics and leans the wrong way. The weight of the boat shifts dramatically and we start to roll. Miranda and Stacey stop paddling and stare open-mouthed.

We lurch sideways. Noah throws his paddle forward and flops into the water.

I take a deep breath and dive, hoping I can push far enough away from the upturned kayak.

The last sound I hear before going under is mocking laughter.

The water is cold, bracing and murky. I close my eyes in case I see schools of bass, piranha-like, swimming towards me. I come up spluttering and put my feet down to kick myself towards the kayak, floating off slowly downstream.

My feet touch the bottom and I stand.

The water is only chest deep.

Noah flails like a man falling from a towering skyscraper, his arms reaching desperately for something to hold onto. I walk over to him and grip his hands. He realises I'm standing up.

He stands as well.

A kookaburra laughs.

Tim and Braith and twenty-four students join in.

Mr Jackson does the honourable thing and stops our kayak from floating further downstream. I plod to the beach, dripping wet, embarrassed beyond belief.

Shrugging out of my life jacket, I casually say, 'I felt like a swim.'

Tim and Braith howl with laughter.

Tim says, 'Yeah, in the babies pool, Walker.'

He does a theatrical imitation of me and Noah flailing around.

Even Shakespeare would be impressed.

A moment away

The class lazes around on the beach, eating lunch, basking in the afternoon sun, fondly recalling the look of horror on my face as we capsized.

I lie back on my towel and close my eyes, remembering last Saturday, on the back verandah with Dad polishing his football boots. Anything is better than reliving the past hour.

Dad holds a boot up to the light.

'Do ya reckon polishing makes you play better, Dad?'

'I thought it would when I was a kid.'

'Did it?'

'I believed. That was enough.'

'Just believing?'

Dad puts the boot down.

'Saturday morning meant everything to me. Playing with my mates, chasing a ball. The beauty of one diagonal pass.'

He has a faraway look on his face.

'You make it sound religious.'

'It was! It is!'

Dad picks up the brush and starts on the other boot. 'I read somewhere that dentists and accountants have the highest proportion of suicides. And the highest number of evangelical conversions. How's that for a dubious distinction? It's as if we have to believe in something, or else the nothing is too much to bear.'

He shakes his head. 'Well, I don't believe in either of those things. Certainly not topping yourself!'

'And God?'

'Too much myth and pretending.'

Dad makes the sign of the cross with his football boot. 'Give me the purity of one perfect shot, one moment of harmony between me and the ball. That's enough.'

He scoffs at his own sincerity.

'Better to believe in something than nothing at all.'

The backyard, scene of Dad's failed attempts years ago to turn me into a football champion, is covered in morning dew.

'Why didn't football work with me?'

He frowns. 'My fault entirely. Too heavy-handed. I should have been more subtle.'

Dad follows my eyes to the backyard. 'Sons are destined to do the opposite of what their fathers want. I reckon that's a good thing.'

'What did Grandpa want you to do?'

Dad laughs. 'He used to say the same thing, over and over until I got sick of hearing it. A simple philosophy – do the right thing.'

'What the hell . . .'

Dad shakes his head, quickly.

'Think about it, Darcy. Four words.'

'But, how do you know when . . .'

'We know. We just kid ourselves we don't.'

It's too simple, too pat. It's something a parent would say.

'And you live by that?'

Dad scoffs, 'Of course not! I just wish I could.'

A vision of Grandpa sitting in his house, surrounded by memories.

'Do you reckon he liked living alone?'

Dad sighs. 'No. I asked him to come here many times. The stubborn bast— He thought he'd be a burden.'

Dad leans in close. 'I'm not sure how your mum and him would have survived together. They had moments.'

'Why didn't you make him move?'

'Just because he was frail and old, doesn't mean I could do what I wanted.' His voice quivers. 'I argued with him enough.'

He takes a deep breath. 'His independence, that's all he had left. I couldn't take that away.'

We sit quietly for a long time. I notice an old soccer ball, covered in mildew, under the plum tree beside the fence. It's been there, slowly deflating, for ages.

Reaching for Dad's other boot, I hold it out to him,

'You missed a spot. On the toe.'

Dad spits on the boot and polishes intently.

'If you're going to do something, do it right.'

Scroggin

Audrey hands me the plastic bag full of nuts and raisins. She tilts her head back and pops some into her mouth, chewing and speaking at the same time.

'Jacko calls this stuff scroggin.'

'It sounds like something birds do in the undergrowth.'

We both giggle.

She nods toward Noah, sitting on a rock by the river.

'He looks like he's carrying a great weight.'

'It's called a brain.'

'What's your excuse then?'

'Me? I'm still trying to be a man, remember. And failing.'

Audrey leans close.

Apple fragrance overload.

'Saturday night, my backyard. I'll teach you how to meditate. It might help with your . . . issues.'

'Is that a date?'

Audrey smiles. 'Think of it as a meditation class, for free.'

Mr Jackson claps his hands and walks to the river's edge.

'Back to the oars, everybody. Only five kilometres to go. You can sleep on the bus trip home.'

Tim and Braith jump up and run to their boat.

Braith drags it out into the shallows and Tim holds it steady while they both get in. Tim turns to everyone on the beach,

'Hey, Walker, watch and learn. Watch and learn.'

It's pretty tame, even for Tim.

I raise my middle finger but he's already paddling away. Mr Jackson frowns at me.

'It's an old sailor's salute, sir.'

'I'm not stupid, Walker.'

'Yes, sir. I mean, no sir.'

Audrey picks up her life jacket, brushes the sand from it and puts it on. 'When you've mastered meditation, Tim will simply disappear.'

She walks into the shallows, holding the kayak for Claire to climb aboard.

Noah is still sitting on the rock, looking at his reflection in the water. I'm not sure if he's thinking of the boat capsizing or of his father, unshaven, in hospital. I try to picture my dad, unable to move, aimlessly staring across the lounge room, reliving his football games, knowing he'll never play again.

I shiver as I drag the boat into the water, holding it stable.

Noah stands and steps into the stream, grabbing the stern.

'You first, Darcy.'

I have a vision of me stepping in and the boat tipping over again.

'Nah. You jump in, Noah.'

He shakes his head, 'You first, buddy.'

'No chance! I'll hold it steady, Noah.'

'Jump in, Darcy. You're closer.'

'Get in the bloody boat, Noah!'

So much for sensitivity.

Noah carefully hops in and says, 'Kayak, not boat.'

We look at each other and grin.

'More like a bathtub than a kayak, don't ya reckon?'

Inside the tortured mind of young Darcy

The wind picks up and pushes us along.

We stroke evenly and slowly, letting the current do the rest. Occasionally a fish leaps from the river and twirls sunlight silver in mid-air. Cows wander along the bank wondering when someone will stop the war in Afghanistan and whether the Global Financial Crisis will affect the price of milk. They lift their tails and urinate in huge arching torrents, then drop their heads and return to lunch.

Everyone is quiet, hoping the next bend is the last. Miranda and Stacey complain about sore shoulders and blisters on their hands. Tim and Braith are nowhere to be seen. Mr Jackson and Ms Pine try to encourage the group to join in a sing-a-long.

Why are teachers always so optimistic?

Ms Pine has a lovely soft voice. Mr Jackson is monotone. No-one joins in.

Here is a list of my river thoughts, in no particular order.

Audrey.

Yes, I know. Predictable.

I close my eyes and remember every conversation we've had. Then I recall everything she's said in English class. Next, I try meditating.

All I can think of is Audrey in various states of undress.

That's lechery, not mysticism. I feel vaguely obscene and juvenile.

I am obscene and juvenile.

I consciously picture Audrey fully dressed. This is much easier.

Audrey in her school uniform.

Audrey in jeans and white top.

In tracksuit pants and baggy sweater.
In a long black evening gown with a red belt.
Audrey wearing Dunlop Volleys.
In knee-high boots.
In shiny black school shoes.
Audrey in football uniform.

Hang on, where did that come from?

No matter what I do, I can't escape the vision of Audrey wearing Dad's football jersey and shorts. I squeeze my eyes tightly shut, dig my paddle into the water quickly and repetitively, trying to wipe this image.

Audrey is chasing the football now, three burly blokes closing in. The goalkeeper runs towards her to block the shot. The big blokes wear scowls, baggy pants and black shirts. The keeper lunges. Audrey effortlessly chips the ball over his head. All the men collide, the sound of crunching bones and expanded air. Audrey spins away from the mayhem and runs triumphant behind the goal. She sees me by the corner flag and wheels towards me, her arms wide in celebration.

A sports dream with a feminist subtext? An ideologically sound romance? Me and my conscience relax back into the kayak.

A lone donkey stands on a rise overlooking the river. His ears point at odd angles as if he's not sure which way to turn. His tail lazily swats flies. Beyond the next bend, I hear a deep voice making 'hee-haw' noises. Tim is no doubt rehearsing his ass jokes.

'Hey, Noah, what do you want to be when you grow up?'

Noah turns around and giggles. 'You're kidding?'

'No, seriously. Come on, it'll pass the time until our arms drop off.'

Noah stops paddling and looks up at the gum trees lining each bank.

The sun is low in the sky, setting behind the distant ridge. We have enough light for another hour of paddling. Mr Jackson keeps glancing at his watch and looking behind him, as if the river monster is catching up.

'I want to be famous.'

'Famous!'

'Sure, why not. I'll start a legendary company.'

'What sort?'

'I'd like to design the world's first chessboard you can use in space.'

'You want to be an astronaut as well?'

'No. I get sick on planes, but imagine the publicity. Astronauts floating around the cabin yet all the pieces stay in place. Everyone would want a set.'

'For when they go into space?'

Noah's voice is droll. 'No. Because they saw it on television.'

Do we want what we see on TV? Of course, that's why there are advertisements, stupid.

'Noah, why did you throw that snake?'

He doesn't turn around, just paddles a little slower as he thinks.

We men can't do two things at once.

I try to maintain a rhythm but he keeps leaving the paddle in the water and not stroking. The kayak threatens to go in a circle. It's only the current that carries us downstream.

'I wanted to scare Tim. To show he's not so tough. Scared of a little plastic snake.'

He turns and giggles, then looks ahead to the nearest kayak with Mr Jackson and Ms Pine. 'It worked, didn't it?'

'It sure did, Noah.'

'Nerd's revenge, Darcy. Noah the nerd's revenge.'

He giggles again.

'Tim's going to pay you back, you know.'

Noah looks a little guilty and sheepish.

'Then why does he keep picking on you?'

He lowers his voice. 'I reckon he thinks you did it, Darcy. Sorry.'

We paddle in silence for a while, both thinking of Tim beating the plastic snake to death with a burning log.

'Hey, Noah.'

'Yeah.'

'Your dad, he'll pull through.'

Noah doesn't turn around. He grips the paddle a little tighter and pulls faster. We start catching up to Miranda and Stacey.

Noah's voice is quiet. 'At least I'm doing something. Mum just sits at the kitchen table, not saying a word.'

Miranda looks across at us and calls out, 'Hey, you don't have any gloves, do ya?'

She raises her hands, palms outward to show how red and blistered they are.

'Sure. I've got a pair of silk gloves, right here beside the outboard motor. That'll be ten dollars?'

'Ha bloody ha. Loser.'

Noah and me paddle faster as Stacey and Miranda drift. Both have their feet outside the cockpit now, stretching their legs along the kayak. They mournfully look at their hands and pout.

I call back, '*Be not afraid of greatness*, Miranda.'

'Piss off, Shakespeare.'

The sound of shouted voices comes from around the next bend.

Noah and me paddle quickly, eager to finish.

'This time, Noah. Let's beach the boat before we get out, okay?'

'Kayak, Darcy. It's a kayak.'

The kayaks are all lined along a thin stretch of sand up ahead. Everyone is standing on the beach looking towards the weir, where Tim and Braith balance on the concrete wall, the water metres below them.

'Come down, please,' Ms Pine pleads.

'Now means now!' Mr Jackson's voice is firm.

Tim and Braith both have their arms outstretched, like tightrope walkers, as they tentatively inch their way along the wall. Tim cups his hands over his mouth and yells –

'No worries, sir. We just want to reach the other side.'

Mr Jackson yells, 'This is not being part of a team, Harris!'

Tim and Braith turn to face the river. They raise their hands above their heads, preparing to dive.

Submerged rocks.

Splattered brains.

Mr Jackson thunders, 'DO NOT DIVE!'

Tim and Braith shout together, something that sounds suspiciously like a Tarzan call. Not words, just a Neanderthal holler.

They stretch their arms out wide in front of them, chests expanded like obsessive body-builders.

Ms Pine screams, 'No!'

They dive majestically out from the wall. Half-way down, they break from their perfect arched-back head-down posture. Tim pulls his knees up to his chest, closes his eyes and yells 'Cowabunga!' His dive partner curls up into a Braith-size ball, head tucked tightly to his chest, arms wrapped around his knees. They both hit the water with a thud, slabs of concrete dropped from a great height.

Bubbles.
 Screams from the beach.
 Swearing from Mr Jackson.
 More bubbles.

Noah and I paddle as fast as we can to where they landed. We reach the spot in a few seconds. Sludge and soupy water – and Tim's ugly mug rising like a wrinkled turtle right beside my paddle.

 I could smack him once in the neck and he'd sink, quicker than a stone.

 Braith surfaces a few seconds later on the opposite side of the kayak. Both of them are spluttering water and laughing. They see the looks of concern on our faces and laugh even louder. The paddle feels like a scythe in my sweaty palms.

 Just one swipe.

Mr Jackson calls from the bank, 'You two, out of the water at once!'

I assume he means the diving twins, but Noah and me paddle to the bank, just in case. All the girls crowd along the beach watching Tim and Braith stroke slowly and easily back to the bank.

Noah and me flap behind in our boat.

Sorry, kayak.

The return of the sodden sailors

On the beach opposite the weir, we pack our drenched gear into plastic bags and tip the kayaks upside down to drain. Mr Jackson utters the word 'detention' a record twenty-two times. Braith and Tim snicker, basking in the adoration of Stacey and Miranda.

The jungle-green duo arrive in their truck and begin loading the kayaks aboard. The hairy one seems unnaturally interested in talking to Audrey instead of doing his work. He has a tattoo of a snake coiled around a heart on his bicep. Audrey ignores him and sits on her daypack, waiting for the bus. She stares into the distance as snake-man flexes his muscles and lifts her kayak onto the trailer singlehandedly.

'Good trip?' he asks.

Audrey nods and looks towards me, bless her.

That's all the invitation I need.

Dragging my kayak across to the trailer, I drop it near snake-man. He looks at me and grins, 'Hello, sailor. Didn't fall in too often?' He looks in my kayak. 'Enough water in here to drown a rat.'

He turns the kayak over, water splashes over his Adidas trainers. He skips out of the way a second too late.

My voice is mock-friendly, 'That's not water, mate. It's urine. My partner had an accident.'

Snake man looks up quickly.

'Very funny, Sonny.'

He says the last word with a sneer.

Then he calls across to his partner to help him with the kayak, just in case any more water should splash out.

The bus rumbles down the bush track, Frank Sinatra blasting out.

Audrey stands and shoulders her backpack.

I smile at snake-man, 'Thanks for letting us use your canoes.'

'Kayaks, you prick.'

And so ends the adventure down the Kangaroo River.

We board the bus for home. Tim and Braith, the next Olympic diving champions, lounge across the back seat. Me and Noah and the chessboard are down the front and Audrey is alone a few seats behind. Noah opens the chess game and selects the white pawns.

'That was fun, Darcy.'

I reach for the black pieces.

'As much fun as a hatful of assholes.'

Noah giggles. 'Where did you learn that one?'

'My grandpa.'

'Can I use it? It might get a response from Dad. He liked – likes – stupid sayings.'

Noah frowns. 'But not swear words.'

'Asshole isn't swearing. It's an anatomical description.'

Noah looks quickly behind. 'Yeah, of Tim's face.'

He moves pawn to e4.

Me and Dad have a serious talk

Saturday night in the bathroom. On the mirror, I draw a steamy love heart, my face framed within.

Dad knocks on the door outside.

'Are you okay, Darcy?'

'Fine, Dad. I'm shaving.'

Actually I'm trying to see myself as Audrey will in exactly twenty-five minutes.

Is that a fresh blackhead sprouting aggressively from the tip of my nose or a smudge on the mirror?

I wipe the mirror, breaking the heart.

My fingers leave a trace of oil; the blackhead remains.

I open the cabinet and look through Mum's cosmetics, trying to decide between . . .

Revlon Age Defying Makeup?
Blackhead?
Beyond Natural Smoothing Primer?
Blackhead?
Translucent Finishing Powder with Botafirm?
Blackhead?
The Age Defying Makeup is $37.95 for 37 mls. At that price, I should look sixteen until I'm a grandfather.

Let's go with a naked blackhead, shall we?

Cupping my hands under the tap, I rinse my face, applying a strong layer of almond scrub, $4.95 from KMart. It contains one almond, a greasy paste that could be flour and water and five hundred grams of tiny grains – from a grain farm?

I follow the instructions to *rub vigorously while counting to fifty, then rinse.*

A slightly red fresh face stares back at me, with a blackhead on its nose.

Dad knocks again.

'Have you cut yourself, Darcy?'

'Yeah, both wrists, Dad.'

Silence.

'Darcy?' Dad's voice is strained. He's going to have to break the door down to rescue me. Right now he's bracing his shoulder hoping he has enough strength to force the lock. Or he's walking out to the shed for the axe. He's praying it doesn't come to that. Too much noise, too much damage.

'You are okay, aren't you, son?'

I open the door and Dad stumbles inside. He'd had his ear to the keyhole, listening for mumbled groans and cries for help.

'It's a blackhead, Dad. Not enough to kill myself over.'

He grins and tousles my hair.

'Please don't rub your dirty hands in my hair, Dad.'

He follows me to the kitchen, watches as I pour myself a tall glass of milk, smiles when I add two heaped teaspoons of Milo.

'You've been doing that since you were five years old, Darcy.'

He sits at the kitchen table and offers me a chair.

He wants to talk.

Mum is at her book club. Every second Saturday a few women from her office meet to discuss the latest in world literature.

Mum had gathered her car keys and handbag and this fortnight's novel — it had a shiny red cover with a dagger plunging into a tree.

Crime.

Doesn't she get enough of that at work?

Mum kissed me and nodded seriously at Dad, whispering, 'Don't forget.'

Dad clears his throat.

'Darcy.'

I sit opposite, trying to remove the dregs of crunchy Milo from the bottom of the glass.

'Dad.'

'I need to talk to you about something.'

'I know.'

'You know? How? Did your Mum tell you?'

We look at each other for a minute, trying to work out who knows what.

That's easy.

We both know nothing.

'I know you want to talk to me, but I don't know what about.' Trying to make light of the situation, I add, 'Sex, probably.'

Dad looks quickly toward the door as if Mum may have heard, even though she left twenty minutes ago.

'You do know?'

Now I'm totally confused.

'What the hell are you on about, Dad?'

He flinches at my tone. I didn't mean to yell, but I have a date in — I glance at my watch — fifteen minutes.

'Sex.'

I look up quickly.

'Pardon.'

'Sex, son. I need to talk to you about sex.'

'Why?'

Dad breathes deeply and sighs.

'Because your mother told me to.'

'Why?'

'Because I'm your father and she thinks it's time.'

'Why?'

'Darcy, can you stop saying "why"?'

Dad rubs his face with both hands, trying to wake himself out of this nightmare.

This is my sex talk. I must be very preoccupied to take so long to understand.

'It's okay, Dad. I know about sex.'

'How?'

Is he asking for proof?

'I just do, that's all.'

'You mean from books and — the internet.'

Now is not the time to talk with Dad about science

books; biology classes; porn sites and fumblings at Stacey's.

'Trust me, Dad. I know stuff.'

Shakespeare rolls restlessly in his grave.

Dad leans back in his chair and looks around the kitchen. His eyes settle on the photos of me on the opposite wall.

My first day of school wearing a bright yellow hat.

Me at the beach sitting under an umbrella.

Me on a pony at the fair, Dad leading it around the oval.

He sighs again, 'Your mum says I've got to tell you stuff, even if you claim to know it.'

That sounds like Mum, no stone unturned.

Ten minutes to go. Do blackheads itch? I dare not touch my nose and make it worse.

'You win, Dad. Tell me about sex.'

Dad flinches again at the mention of the word.

He looks at his hands fiddling with the tablecloth. 'Okay.'

He takes a deep breath and repeats, 'Okay.'

'I'll use a condom, Dad. If I have sex any time in the next fifty years, I'll use a condom. How's that?'

'Perfect! A condom is good.'

He looks around the kitchen, searching for inspiration.

'And I'll be respectful and courteous and I won't force myself on anybody.'

'That's good too.'

He looks again towards the door, expecting Mum to walk in and remind him of something he's forgotten. He smiles awkwardly.

'Is that it, Dad? I've got to go.'

'Your Mum said I should mention . . . um . . . satisfaction.'

'What!'

'She said young men should know things, should be told things so that the girl won't be . . .' his eyes plead for understanding, '. . . disappointed.'

I'd be ecstatic to hold Audrey's hand tonight! Mum and Dad have us both . . .

It's hard not to giggle.

'No worries, Dad. My biology teacher said I was a natural.'

Dad looks confused.

'I'm kidding, Dad.'

He gets up from the chair and walks to the fridge, takes out a bottle of wine and fills a pint beer tumbler.

He takes a hearty sip.

'Okay. That's over. Fair enough?'

'Sure, Dad.' I stand and give him a quick hug. Poor bloke, having to do the dirty work while Mum's off with her gang.

'Dad? What did Grandpa tell you about sex?'

'He said if I got a girl pregnant, he'd kill me.'

A quick detour

Back in the bathroom, I study the smeared heart. Me and the blackhead are still partners. A branch of the wattle tree scrapes on the windowpane, tiny fingers pawing the glass. A willy-wagtail lands on the branch and whistles at the insect on my nose.

'It's a minor blemish, okay!'

He flies off in search of smaller prey.

Audrey is changing into her meditation clothes, standing thoughtfully in front of her bedroom mirror, not freaked out by blemishes and bad skin. Her parents are not conducting long lectures on the pleasures and dangers of sex.

Bugger Mum and Dad. They've got me thinking about it. Parents are not supposed to encourage their sons that way!

I'll need all the meditation I can get.

Now one word keeps thrashing about in my head.

One awful teenage-boy word.

Condom.

Visions of Tim and Braith tossing packets of them in the air at Stacey's parties. Everyone scattering from the dance floor as 'Sexual Healing' blares from the speakers. Braith making obscene gestures with his hips. Tim opening a condom and blowing it up, balloon-size, tying it in a knot and bouncing it on Marcus's head. And when it bursts, Tim yells 'pinhead' over and over at Marcus until he seeks sanctuary beside me in the kitchen. I offer him a glass and tell him it's pink lemonade. Marcus drinks it down in one gulp and asks for another.

Reaching for my mobile, I text Audrey that I'll be thirty minutes late.

She texts straight back that she'll 'start without me.'

The chemist first. Better safe than sorry.

Grabbing my wallet and keys, I leave through the backdoor, calling out 'bye' to Dad. He yells, 'Have fun.'

On the street, the power lines over my head hum with tension. A light breeze tickles my scalp.

Why am I sweating?

The dry leaves are bunched along the footpath. They crunch and snap and pop like breakfast cereal. At Southey Street, I wait for the traffic lights to change, remembering holding Dad's hand on the way home from kindergarten, calling out for the green man, eager to reach the shops where we'd buy ice creams and sit in the park opposite, giggling and licking as they melted.

Dad always ordered vanilla. My favourite was caramel and chocolate, double scoop.

I'd rather buy an ice cream now as the middle-aged woman in a white uniform and chemist's badge approaches me.

'Can I help you, young man?'

Did she just place extra emphasis on the word 'young'?

'I'm fine, thanks. Just looking.'

Yes, I'm searching for a jar of Brylcreem for Clegg. Or shopping for Christmas on a Saturday night in September.

The lady smiles briefly. 'Well, call me for assistance.'

A voice in my head pleads, 'He needs all the help he can get.'

Dad's voice reassures, 'Leave him alone, he's fine.'

I wander nervously among the endless jars of vitamins; rows of herbal tonics; cartons of flu tablets; and the limitless choice of shampoo and conditioners.

Until I reach aisle five, midway down,

Ecstasy

Bliss

Paradise

Pleasure

and

Sensation.

Who comes up with these names? And which pack has the least condom-like appearance? Blue and white stripes and the word *Sensation* written in big letters. Much better than the hot red packs with pictures of moaning women, promising the rubbers inside have special powers. I walk slowly to the counter, hoping for a male assistant on duty. The same woman smiles from behind the register and reaches for my packet to scan. In a loud voice, she says, 'That's five dollars sixty for a pack of three. Will there be anything else?'

Lubricant?

Sex aids?

Viagra?

Blushing to the tip of my blackhead, I give her the exact money. She pops the packet into a brown paper bag and hands it across the counter. My hand is shaking. She doesn't notice. The lady is the same age as Mum. Does she demand her husband have sex chats with their children?

Probably not a good time to ask her.

She says 'thank you' and moves to the next customer, an old man buying bulk vitamins. He fumbles in his wallet for the money and coins drop onto the shiny tiled floor. I reach down to pick them up. He squints at me as I hand them over. 'Thank you, young lady.'

Is my hair that long?

I walk out of the shop as casually as a teenager carrying a full packet of condoms. My knees are shaking and a vein throbs in my neck. I make the doorway without running, looking left and turning right and . . .

whack

walk straight into a brick wall.

Well, somebody *built* like a brick wall.

The paper bag drops at his feet as I try to stay upright. He grunts and holds his head. Reaching forward, I touch his arm, saying sorry, over and over.

Tim Harris rubs his head and looks straight at me, taking a few seconds to work out what's happened.

It was a brick wall!

Tim shakes his head. 'What the hell!'

'It's me, Tim. Darcy.'

Surely he can't be that hurt. It was only my elbow and his head.

'Why did you hit me, Walker?'

'I didn't.' I hold up my elbow to show him.

'It was an accident. I wasn't watching where I was going. Sorry.'

How many times should I say sorry? Once more, and than a quick getaway?

He looks at the paper bag in my hand.

'What are they? Condoms?'

'Very funny, Tim.'

I offer him the paper bag, nonchalantly. 'You want to share?'

He looks quickly up and down the street.

'I'm not gay, you know. I can buy my own. Not that I'm buying condoms. I'm just . . .' He looks up the street, 'I'm on my way to the kebab shop.'

I blame the shock of running into Tim for what I said next.

'I'll walk with you. It's on my way home.'

Tim grimaces, like he's been offered cat food instead of chicken kebab.

'Yeah, right.'

He strides ahead, leaving me no alternative but to tag along or stand holding a packet of condoms at the entrance to the chemist, where I can auction them to the highest bidder.

Single mums with strollers.

Too late there.

An old lady with a walking stick and a jaunty polka-dot floppy hat sitting at the bus stop.

Definitely not.

Tim turns to me. 'You coming, Walker?'

'Sure.'

Tim smells of Brut 33 and his hair sticks up in a thousand different directions like an anteater casually dropped on his skull. His trousers flop around oversize Converse shoes, laces undone. His big hands burrow deep into his pockets.

'What are you doing tonight, Walker? Not that I care.'

'Very gentlemanly of you to ask, Tim. I have a . . .' Oops, I almost said date.

'An assignment due on Monday.'

He looks at me, pityingly.

'Saturday night at home, hey?'

He saunters along, glad somebody is a bigger loser than him.

He lowers his voice.

'I've got a date.'

'Yeah, who with?'

'Miranda . . .' he waits for a few seconds and then adds, 'and Stacey.'

What does he expect me to say?

'Where's Braith?'

'I don't need Braith to hold my hand, mate.'

We walk past the fish and chips shop, the Reject Shop, the florist, the newsagent and the hairdresser. Tim points at a picture in the hairdresser window, a guy with a mohawk and shaved sides.

'I might get one like that.'

'Great. You can play Cowboys and Indians, like when you were a kid.'

Tim grins. 'You're right. It's a crap haircut.'

Tim Harris has just agreed with something I've said.

I'm speechless.

Well, almost …

'Tim, why did you dive off the weir?'

He laughs, remembering the looks on everyone's faces.

'To see the looks on everyone's faces.'

This is getting seriously scary! Harris is thinking like me. Or, I'm thinking like him!

He grins and I see something unexpected in his eyes. It's humour – innocent boyish humour from bonehead Tim.

'You should have seen Jacko. He grabbed Ms Pine by the arm when me and Braith jumped. His career drowning before his eyes.'

'How did you know the water was deep enough?'

Tim studies his reflection in the shop window, patting the anteater.

'It had to be pretty deep, being near the wall.'

He smirks. 'We didn't even touch the bottom.'

'You wouldn't be walking around if you did.'

He looks from his reflection to me.

'You know, Walker, you can be a killjoy sometimes.'

'Sure can. But one with his own hands and arms and body. All in working order.'

Tim shrugs. 'Nothing ventured . . .'

He tries to recall the rest of the saying then gives up.

He reaches across and lightly punches my arm. 'You have fun studying tonight, Walker.'

He turns to go.

'Hey, Tim.'

'Yeah.'

'It was a pretty good dive.'

He waits for me to add some smartass remark. I don't.

'Thanks, Walker.'

He struts into the kebab shop, checking out the menu on the wall. Tim's big night out.

And mine too.

The . . . date

Somewhere a lawn mower spits gravel and whines. A troupe of homing pigeons pirouette across the sky and fold in unison towards old man Smit's cages. He pours seed into the gutters, whistling them home. Rebecca Hart plays on a swing in the front yard, Mrs Hart watching from the kitchen window. Pete and Randall Finch, in stubbies and singlets, sit on the front step of their house, listening to football on the radio.

A young man walks nervously down the street.

Slow down.

Don't sweat.

Don't get flustered.

I remove one condom from the packet and place it in my wallet, underneath the student card. I casually saunter past my house, dropping the condom packet into our letterbox. Dad won't check the mail on Saturday night. Even he has better things to do.

I try whistling as I reach Audrey's front gate. The sound comes out thin and dribbly, like a baby blowing raspberries. The front garden is overgrown with native shrubs and rock gardens. On each side of the stairs is a naked female statue; both have unnaturally large breasts. One statue has a snail slowly slithering up her leg.

At the dark timber front door, I cross my eyes, trying desperately to see the blackhead on the tip of my nose.

Audrey opens the door before I've knocked.

Before I've uncrossed my eyes.

'Nice face, Darcy.'

Think of the brightest colour red you can imagine. Call it blush red.

'Come in. Mum and Dad aren't home. It's the anniversary of their first date!'

Audrey walks to the kitchen and I follow, hands in my pockets to stop them shaking.

'How many years?'

'Mum reckons twenty-four, Dad says twenty-three. They were arguing about it when they left.' Audrey frowns. 'Maybe they'll be home earlier than expected.'

'Great.'

'Great?'

'Sorry! I mean . . . I mean it's great they've been together so long.'

'You want a coffee?'

'Before meditating?'

Audrey giggles and pulls herself up to sit on the kitchen bench. She's wearing tight black pants, a dark green top and matching ballet shoes. No socks.

Don't look at her ankles!

'We don't have to meditate, Darcy, I just wanted to ask you over.'

I stand like an empty-handed delivery boy in the middle of the room, not sure who stole my pizza. Audrey pats the bench top beside her. There are six very sturdy wooden chairs around a long kitchen table. I saunter (that is, I don't stumble!) over to her and jump on the bench.

NOT TOO CLOSE!

But close enough for her to see my blackhead.

I blurt out, 'Green is my favourite colour.'

Audrey looks at my grey trousers, black T-shirt and black shoes.

'Your shoes, Audrey. I didn't know you did ballet.'

'I don't. I saw a documentary, ages ago, about Paris. Everyone wore these shoes.'

Audrey reaches down to rub her hand along the soft leather. 'It's as close as I'll get to Paris.'

'Until after Year Twelve.'

Audrey wrinkles her nose. It is perfectly clear of blackheads.

'Don't remind me.'

'I read about the canals of Paris.'

'Isn't that Venice?'

'Paris has them too. With barges that people live on.'

'Could be a problem if you're a sleep water?'

'Did you say "sleep water", or "walker"?'

Audrey giggles, 'Sleepwalker who ends up in the water. Do you sleepwalk?'

'Nah, I just sweat in strange places.'

'You mean strange places, like Paris or Venice?'

'And Verona, underneath Juliet's balcony.'

'*Romeo, Romeo, wherefore art thou Romeo?*'

Is the girl of my dreams quoting Shakespeare back at me?

Perchance, to dream.

Our legs are two centimetres from touching on the bench. How long can I sit this near to Audrey without shaking? In an effort to stop thinking of how close we are, I focus on the toaster at the end of the bench.

'Why are you looking at our toaster, Darcy?'

'I'm wondering if Shakespeare ever wrote about toast?'

'Parting is such sweet . . . toast!'

'Double, double toil and . . . toast!'

'Friends, Romans, countrymen, lend me your . . . toasters!'

'Audrey, how do you know so much Shakespeare?'

Audrey giggles. 'I studied.'

'But Ms Hopkins hasn't set anything this year.'

'Not for school, for . . .' Audrey blushes. She jumps down from the bench and walks towards the back door, beckoning me to follow. She leads me out to the back garden, heavily planted with native shrubs and more naked statues, male and female. She walks along a gravel path, through the naturalist orgy, to a tartan blanket spread out on the grass. She sits cross-legged in one corner and I sprawl in the other.

'You like to say the first thing that comes into your head, don't you, Darcy?'

'Not if I can help it.'

Audrey looks reproachfully at me.

I nod, 'Yeah, I can't help myself.'

'Have you ever played "word association"? You'd be an expert.'

'Is that where someone says a word and I say "sex" back?'

Did I really just say the 'S' word to Audrey?

I look to the night sky for help. The stars grin back, inanely.

'Only if you must, Darcy.'

It can't get more embarrassing, can it?

Audrey sits up straight, fine laughter lines around her eyes.

Is it too dark for her to see my blackhead?

Audrey begins, 'Come on, let's try. I say a word, you respond. Okay?'

'Shoot.'

She looks up into the night sky.

'Stars.'

'*The fault, dear Brutus, is not in our stars.*'

'No more Shakespeare!'

'At least I didn't say "sex"!'

'Darcy, stop saying "sex"!'

'Okay, the next person to say "sex" has to –'

Audrey puts her hands on her hips. 'Has to stop saying it!'

'Fair enough.'

'Let's try again. No Shakespeare, no s– You know. Ready ...

'Clothes.'

'Dirty.'

'Music.'

'S ... S ... soothing.'

'That was close. Picnic.'

'Bull ants.'

'What?'

'Bull ants. When I was a kid we went on a picnic and I got stung by hordes of bull ants. Dad took me to hospital and the nurse covered all the bites with sticky pink cream.'

Audrey shakes her head, 'You really are – unique.'

'You were going to say something else then?'

'Let's do as many as possible, quickly. No stopping.'

'And no sex.'

'Darcy!'

'Sorry. Go ahead.'

'Grass.'

'Stacey's parties.'

'Kayak.'

'Canoe.'

'Noah.'

178

'And the seven dwarves.'

Audrey giggles.

'This is not called "finish my sentence by saying something silly", Darcy. It's meant to be single-word association.'

'I couldn't resist. I should have said, Noah and the seven chess pieces.'

'He is a little obsessed, isn't he?'

'He's focused. I like him. He's persistent – and different.'

'Well, if you like him, I do too.'

'That's a little wishy-washy.'

I've just called the girl of my dreams wishy-washy!

Audrey ignores me. 'Lonely.'

'Friendly.'

'Sad.'

'Sack.'

'Beautiful.'

'Waste.'

Audrey looks surprised.

I add, 'It's a song, "Beautiful Waste" by The Triffids.'

'I know! My mum plays that song over and over.'

'I have the same taste as your mother?'

Audrey pats my knee. 'I love that song too. Mum and Dad used to follow the band when they were young. The singer died.'

'Yeah, I know. Just like Jim Morrison. Only he could sing and write decent songs.'

'Who? Jim Morrison?'

'No. The singer from The Triffids. David McComb.'

'Do you know Jim Morrison is buried in Paris?'

'Anywhere near the canal?'

'He's in a cemetery full of famous people. They have to keep a guard at his gravesite. People scrawl messages to him. As if he can read them, from underground.'

'I don't believe in it, sorry.'

'What, writing messages to dead people?'

'No, dead people reading those messages. You just die and rot and the only thing that lives on is your spirit in other people. Your mum and dad and friends.'

'Can your spirit read the messages through them?'

'No. Your friends can. But they wouldn't like people writing on your grave. So they wouldn't tell your spirit about it.'

Audrey shakes her head. 'If your spirit exists in other people, they couldn't hide stuff like graffiti on a gravestone. They'd be offended on behalf of your spirit.'

It makes sense to me. 'But would they wash the graffiti off? Or never visit your grave again?'

Audrey brushes the hair from in front of her face. 'If you were really famous, your true friends wouldn't go to your grave in the first place. They couldn't stand the crowds. They'd choose a special place where you both shared something and they'd go there. They'd take flowers. Or have a picnic, spread the blanket out, lie back, look at the sky and remember.'

I quickly look down at the blanket and then up at the stars.

'No-one is buried here, Darcy. The spirits aren't out tonight.'

'Spirits are always out. It's whether we see them or not.'

Audrey leans across and kisses me on the lips. So quickly I don't have time to feel nervous or embarrassed or excited. I close my eyes and kiss back.

'What was that for?'

'For believing in spirits,' Audrey winks, 'and for fun.'

'What happened to our word game, Audrey.'

'That kiss just scared it away.'

'Never to return?'

'Never. Too much sex.'

'I only said it once or twice.'

Audrey smiles. 'Is it true?'

'Is what true?'

'About boys and sex. How they're meant to think of it every thirty seconds, or something ridiculous like that.'

I shake my head. 'No way. We think of it much more than that!'

Audrey giggles. 'Do you have room for anything else?'

I'm tempted to tell her how I can recite *Romeo and Juliet*.

Audrey clicks her fingers. 'What?'

'What, what?'

'You were thinking of something then. I could tell.'

'Somebody is always thinking of something, Audrey.'

'You mean "everybody is always thinking of something".'

'Yeah. With men it's sex, with women it's ...'

Audrey smiles and looks towards her house, 'We're never silly enough to admit what we think about.'

'I'd hate to know what everyone was thinking. It would be depressing. Imagine getting really involved in Ms Hopkins's class and then discovering she's preoccupied with watering her roses when she gets home. Or she's planning to join the Liberal Party. Or she likes . . .'. I shiver, 'football.'

'Do you have a crush on Ms Hopkins?'

'Of course not. But it'd be awful to find out someone you admire thinks dull boring dreary thoughts.'

'She is very attractive, Darcy.'

'I like her T-shirts, okay!'

'You're full of it, Walker.'

'You sounded like Clegg then!'

'Nobody sounds like Clegg!'

We both look at each other and it's the closest I'll ever come to an 'I'm centre of the universe' moment.

Audrey leans forward.

I don't think she wants to shake my hand.

Walking after midnight

Audrey and me have been in the backyard for hours, discussing how all the yellow beanbags in the seniors common room smell like perfume and the blue ones smell like rotting peaches. And how, after Stacey's parties, Miranda Fry always wears a high-neck top to school under her uniform, no matter what the temperature. How most religions don't seem to like women much. How vegans must get really nervous every time they chop the head off a carrot or an onion. Can they hear the vegetables scream?

And what must it feel like to be a stick of celery slowly lowered into a juicer, the blades whirring madly?

And who came up with the word 'topography'? Or 'lexicon'?

And why is cricket a boring game played by overweight men in white clothes and the name of a small insect?

Audrey looks at her watch.

'I reckon Mum and Dad have kissed and made up.'

'Parents do that. It shows they're mature or ...'

'... Or have no alternative!'

Audrey stretches her legs and winces. 'My bottom is as numb as a frog in a fridge.'

She stands and offers to help me up and I wipe my hand on my trousers before reaching out.

'Are you worried about giving me boy germs?'

'Sweat, remember.'

'Oh yeah, the boy who sweats in strange places.'

Audrey reaches for my hand, even though I'm standing on my two relatively steady feet. She leads me down the path.

'Why so many naked statues, Audrey?'

'Dad says it's better than swans made out of car tyres and dwarves in red costumes. Do you want to go for a walk?'

'Only if you keep holding my hand.'

Audrey smiles, the tiniest gap between her front teeth.

When we reach the gate, Audrey turns left and I head right, away from my house. Our hand-holding stretches . . . we look at each other . . . and Audrey relents, '*Lay on, Macduff.*'

'We'll take it in turns. You choose at the next corner.'

'We may end up going in circles.'

'Like a drunk on Saturday night. Which reminds me, I saw Tim earlier.'

'Did he want a fight?'

'We got on okay. It felt a little weird.'

'Where did you see him?'

'Outside the chem—'

The first lesson of hiding the truth is to not blurt it out. The second lesson is to not stop half-way through blurting it out.

'– At the shops.'

Audrey looks enquiringly. 'What are you hiding, Darcy?'

'I'm not hiding nothing. Anything. Or something!'

Audrey holds up our hands, still clasped together. I ask, 'What?'

'I was checking how many fingers you've crossed for lying.'

The streetlight shines on me like in those spy movies where the villain is under interrogation. *Not the light! Anything but the light!*

'I ran into Tim at the chemist.'

A gentle rain begins to drift across the beam of the streetlight. A man with menacing scars in a long coat and black hat reaches for the bamboo to shove under my fingernails.

I whisper, 'I was buying condoms.'

There are droplets of rain on Audrey's hair, 'Was that what you were slipping into your letterbox?'

'How did you . . .?'

'I was watching. Sorry. I was so nervous about tonight.'

'*You* were nervous?'

'Sure. I thought you might be only interested in meditation. Or you'd be really boring and I wouldn't know how to get you to leave, or you'd try something – something rude.'

'With condoms at the ready!'

'A whole packet!'

Audrey brushes the drops from her face and reaches up to kiss me.

Under the harmless streetlight.

A car horn sounds from across the road. Audrey's mum leans out the car window. 'You'll be home soon, won't you, dear.'

Audrey grips my hand tightly. 'Mum! Go home.'

Audrey's mum looks at me and smiles weakly.

I say, 'Happy anniversary, Mrs Benitez.'

She looks up at the rain coming down heavier. 'It's raining.'

I reply, 'Only outside.'

Audrey giggles. 'We're going for a walk. I won't be long.'

Mrs Benitez glances at the rain again and winds up the window. Audrey and I watch the car roll slowly down the street, turning into their driveway.

Audrey says, 'Did you really tell my mum that it only rains outside?'

'I couldn't think of what to say.'

'I'll spend tomorrow convincing them I'm not going out with a moron.'

'You're not going out with a moron. But you are going out with me?'

'Sure. Why not. If that's okay?'

Audrey Benitez, girl of my dreams, has just asked if it's okay we go out together. And she's still holding my hand. And the rain is making her hair go curly and soft and magical and not even Shakespeare could write such a perfect scene.

'Darcy?'

'Yeah?'

Audrey squeezes my hand. 'You didn't answer me?'

'Oh.'

Audrey acts to kick me in the ankle. 'I repeat, do you want to go out with me?'

'Yes. Definitely. Absolutely. Positively.'

'Good, now can we get out of this rain.'

She leads me across the road to the row of shops. A cat jumps up on a rubbish bin and reaches into the scraps with one dainty paw. A soft-drink can rolls off the pile and clatters onto the footpath. The cat springs to the ground and scampers across the road. We stand outside the supermarket, under the awning, watching the light rain fall. All the shops are closed. Above us a fleet of kamikaze bugs hurtle against the fluorescent lights. They bounce off and flutter drunkenly for a few seconds before trying again. We walk slowly down the street, looking in every shop window. In the shoe shop, a sign reads, *Kumfs $60.*

Audrey says, 'They're for old people – who like the colour beige.'

The next shop is a laundry advertising five collared shirts and two trousers ironed for fifteen dollars. Same-day service.

Audrey suggests, 'It's for single men who can't be bothered.'

'My dad irons his shirts. And Mum's clothes too. He sets up in front of the telly and watches the football, waving the iron around like a loony every time his team scores.' Silence.

'I'm still saying the first thing that comes into my head, aren't I?'

'It's okay. I'm used to it already.'

The next shop is the chemist. There's a picture of a smiling mum and a naked baby underneath an advertisement for nappies.

Audrey says, 'We definitely don't need them,' she looks at me, meaningfully, 'because Darcy's got condoms!'

I blush. 'Leave my condoms alone!'

'I like the word *condom*, it's got a life of its own.'

'Just like what it covers.'

Audrey stops walking and drops my hand.

'Did you just tell a dirty joke?'

Is it possible to pump that much blood into my face?

'I think I did. Sorry.'

Audrey reaches for my hand and our fingers entwine. The word 'condom' disappears from my vocabulary.

The next window is the Reject Shop, red signs plastered all over the glass, displaying one word, *Sale*.

I ask, 'What sort of person shops here?'

'Me!'

'You?'

'Yeah sure. Pens and paper. CDs of disco hits from the seventies. And where do you think Dad gets his garden statues from?'

We reach the corner and both look up at the night sky. The rain has stopped, a few stars are flickering. The road is shiny under the streetlights, a fingernail moon tilts behind a row of houses.

Audrey looks at her watch again. 'I'd better go home.'

We walk slowly down our street. The grass on the footpath is wet and glistening. I've never noticed this before, but each house has a white painted timber fence, except mine and Audrey's. My fence is painted light blue. Audrey's house has a hedgerow of natives, low and dark green.

We stop at my gate.

Audrey reaches up and we kiss, long and slow.

As if on cue, we let go of each other's hand.

Audrey smiles. 'See you tomorrow. After I talk to my parents about you.'

I step over the gate and walk slowly along the path.

Audrey whistles, softly, 'Darcy.'

She points at the letterbox. 'Haven't you forgotten something?'

I plod back to the letterbox and retrieve the packet, holding them up for her to see. She smiles and walks away.

Green is still my favourite colour.

Breakfast with the parents

Before sleeping, I lie in bed looking at the photo of Year Eleven on my dresser. Audrey is in the front row, third from the left, me and Noah on either side of the middle row, like gawky bookends. At the back, Tim is deliberately pulling a stupid face just as the photographer clicks.

We all laughed when we saw the photo a week later. Harris was called to the office and given a lecture about appropriate behaviour, just like last year, and the year before that.

I close my eyes and picture Audrey, in her bed, in green pyjamas.

Dad opens the door and pokes his head in early, way too early, in the morning.

'You awake, Darcy.'

Silence.

'You awake, son.'

Silence.

'Breakfast is ready. Mum's made pancakes with maple syrup.'

'I'm asleep, Dad.'

'Yeah, I know. But pancakes are too good to miss.'

He gently closes the door.

Blackhead inspection time.

Yep, still there. Larger and darker.

In the shower, the cool water wakes me. I dress quickly, smelling the sweet tang of the syrup and the extra butter Mum uses to get the pancakes crispy and light and golden.

Mum and Dad both smile inanely when I walk into the kitchen. Dad reaches across and turns off the radio. They look at me.

'What?'

Mum pours a coffee, 'Nothing, dear.'

Dad adds a heaped teaspoon of sugar to his cup and stirs noisily.

'You were late home, Darcy.'

'Yeah.'

I sit down and reach for the pancakes. The top one is golden brown.

Mum and Dad aren't eating. They both sit, knife and fork poised, waiting for me to talk.

I repeat, 'Yeah.'

Mum rolls her eyes. 'Come on, Darcy. Your father wants to know what happened.'

'Okay. I'll tell him later.'

Dad snickers. He pats Mum's hand.

'Don't worry, dear. I'll report everything.' Then he winks at me. 'Unless Darcy tells me not to.'

'Do you like the pancakes?'

'Yes, Mum.'

She pushes the bottle of maple syrup closer to my plate, a thin smile on her lips. 'I made them especially for you, Darcy.'

Better to get it over with now, so I can enjoy breakfast.

'Me and Audrey went for a walk. That's all. We sat in her backyard and . . .'

Mum raises her eyebrows.

'And meditated.'

Dad nearly chokes on his pancake; he turns away from the table and coughs, holding his hand over his mouth, his eyes squeezed shut. Mum casts an exasperated glance towards him but he's too involved in coughing to notice.

'Okay, Dad. Don't die. I made up the bit about meditating. We talked. Audrey's cool.'

Mum looks from Dad to me and back to Dad.

'Did you and your father have a constructive talk last night?'

Dad wants to cough again, but sees Mum's steely glance and stops himself.

'The sex talk?'

Dad now seems keenly interested in stirring his coffee cup.

Mum reaches across and touches Dad's hand. He stops stirring. He looks out the window instead. This is almost as painful as last night.

'Yes, Mum. Dad told me everything. He's very knowledgeable.'

Dad sits up in his chair, like a schoolboy given a special award for Maths. He smiles at Mum, as if to say *I told you so*.

'Love them and leave them. That's what you said, didn't you, Dad?'

He nods quickly, then realises what I've said.

'I didn't say anything of the sort. Did I?'

He looks pleadingly at me. Mum reaches for the empty plate in the centre of the table. She shakes her head and makes a clicking sound with her tongue, as if to tell us both to stop playing games.

'It's okay, Dad. You were very helpful.'

I look at Mum and say in my most sincere voice, 'Nothing happened, Mum.'

She smiles weakly.

I add, 'At least, not yet.'

'Darcy!'

'Great pancakes, Mum. Any left in the oven?'

Dad tries a weak joke, 'That better be all in the oven, son.'

Mum makes the clicking sound again.

A do-gooder

Audrey wasn't the only person I thought of in bed last night.

I'm not that shallow.

My mind dawdled over to Noah briefly. A vision of him leaning over his father asleep on the lounge chair, handkerchief tucked under his collar. Noah had a can of shaving lotion in one hand and a razor in the other. Should he wake his dad or try and shave him while he sleeps? Noah can't decide. He looks at his dad's chest, rising and falling lightly as he snores.

Then I drifted off into dribble-land and dreamt about Audrey. Nothing too pathetic or tragic. One dream had Audrey and me having a picnic underwater. Clown fish, turtles and dolphins cruised languidly by as we floated along on a shimmering carpet of seagrass waving in the current. Between us was a huge bowl of cherries. Every time I tried to eat one, a moray eel would poke out of the gloom and snatch it away. I got so frustrated I tried punching the eel on the snout.

That was about the time Dad woke me.

Thanks, Dad.

There is precisely three hours and fifty-two minutes before I meet Audrey. Time enough to phone Noah. He answers after one ring, like he's been sitting by the phone waiting.

'Noah?'

'Hello.'

'Hi, it's me, Darcy.'

'Darcy Walker?'

'How many Darcys do you know, Noah?'

What a way to spend Sunday.

'You want a game of chess, Noah? I have a spare . . .' I glance at my watch. 'Three hours and forty-nine minutes.'

Silence.

'Don't worry, Noah. We don't have to play for that long. Just an hour, or two.'

Hell, I don't really want to play at all. I just thought . . .

'You don't want to play, Darcy. You're just trying to be nice.'

'No I'm not.'

'Yes you are.'

'No I'm not . . .'

Silence.

'. . . Okay, even if I am, what else have you got planned today?'

'I got lots to do.'

'Yeah, what?'

This is the second most childish conversation I've ever heard.

'I've got to . . . to do my homework.'

'I rest my case.'

'You don't have to sound so smug, Darcy. You're the one who rang me, remember.'

'Come on, Noah. Just a quick game or two. I'll even let you win.'

He laughs, despite himself. 'You can't stop me winning, Darcy.'

'I'll be over in twenty minutes, okay?'

Silence.

'Okay?'

'Yeah, sure.'

He's acting weird this morning, even for Noah.

Mum and Dad are in the kitchen.

'I'm off. I'll be back for dinner.'

'Don't you have homework?'

'Nah, it's a homework-free weekend, Mum. The school's worried about us getting too stressed.'

She points her finger at me, about to begin cross-examining.

I interrupt, 'I'll do it tonight.'

'Be home by six.'

I mime putting my hand on a stack of Bibles. 'Yes, your honour.'

The clouds look feathery and soft, like in television commercials for airlines where they want you to believe the plane could never crash and, even if it developed engine trouble, it would be held up, miraculously, by all that cotton-wool cumulus.

No-one dies on days like today.

Maybe I'm seeing things differently because of last night?

I'm living in my own ideal television commercial.

I stop for a second on the street corner and close my eyes.

A chorus of sparrows.

A gentle breeze.

The smell of freshly mown grass.

The sweetness of maple syrup lingers on my tongue.

Maybe I am in love? Really really seriously.

And it changes the way I see everything?

When I open my eyes, an Indian couple in a sports car have pulled up in front of me. The lady wears a sari and has a scarf wrapped loosely around her hair. She holds a map out of the window and points at it.

She says, 'The Three Sisters, please?'

It's one of those useless tourist maps that show the main street and have little drawings of all the attractions, clumped together, as if everything you need to see is in town.

The driver leans across. He's wearing a shiny gold watch and has lots of silver chains hanging around his neck. He must jangle and clink when he walks.

He says, 'We've been driving in circles.'

The car smells faintly of incense, sweet and clingy.

The woman smiles.

I want to ask them how long they've been together. If they're married? In love? Ask them to describe the clouds for me. Are they really fluffy white, or just dull grey?

The woman repeats, 'The Three Sisters?'

'Oh, sorry. You take the next left, drive a kilometre, right at the roundabout . . . and follow that for a little way. You can't miss them. They're surrounded by tourists.'

The man puts the car in gear. He checks his mirror to pull out.

The woman leans out of the window and says, 'You looked like you were meditating, just then.'

A vision of Audrey and last night.

She waves as the car speeds away.

Man or amoeba?

Noah lives on a narrow street shaded by tall pine trees on both sides. The wind whistles through them constantly. When I was a kid I was scared of walking down here, believing the whole street was haunted. The trees cast long spindly shadows across the footpath. Noah's house is painted light yellow and one side is covered in dark green creeper. He's sitting on the front verandah, with his dad.

'Hi, Noah. Hi, Mr Hennessy.'

Noah waves. His dad sits in a shiny steel wheelchair, with a pillow at his back. His legs are elevated, resting on a cane coffee table. Mr Hennessy's face is slack and unmoving. His hands are hidden under a crocheted blanket across his lap.

'Dad can't talk yet. But they reckon he will.'

Noah and me sit on the top step. His dad wears red slippers and long dark blue pyjamas, on his wrist is a green plastic band, leftover from the hospital. His hair is neatly combed and he's clean-shaven.

I look at Noah and rub my chin, afraid to say it out loud.

'It's okay, Darcy. The doctors say it's good for Dad to hear voices. He needs . . .'

Noah struggles to remember the doctor's words. 'Social contact.'

'Was it electric, or a razor?'

'Electric. It was pretty easy. I do it every morning. First thing after Dad's wash.'

He looks toward his father.

'It's been two weeks. The doctors say it could change at any time.'

Noah says this in a loud voice, so his Dad can hear. He clicks his fingers to emphasise the point. 'Just like that and Dad could be talking again.'

Mr Hennessy's skin is pale, almost translucent; one side of his mouth sags open, dragged down by renegade muscles. He stares at us for a few seconds, then his gaze falls. Noah gets up and walks to the cushions arranged beside a small table near his dad's chair. The chessboard is open, pieces already set up for the game.

'Me and Dad against you. Fair enough?'

'Easy.'

Noah reaches over and pats his Dad's arm. 'We'll let him make the first move, Dad. He needs all the help he can get.'

Sitting cross-legged on the cushions, I pick up the white knight and open with the Reti gambit, nothing too heroic. Not yet.

Or the next hour as Noah and his dad beat me three games in a row. Before each move, Noah looks up at his dad, to get his approval. Mr Hennessy's eyes give little sign of understanding, but Noah keeps asking. Sometimes he changes his mind about a move, as if some subtle message has passed between father and son. I'm more involved in watching Noah and his dad than the chess.

Maybe that's why I'm losing?

Maybe Noah's dad really is helping?

Noah talks endlessly, sometimes to me, but mainly it's a one-sided monologue on each move with his dad. The third game is the shortest, less than twenty minutes to checkmate. Noah leans across and wipes a small amount of spit from his dad's lips with a hankie and kisses him quickly on the cheek, right in front of me.

'You want a drink, Darcy?'

'Sure. Anything's better than another thrashing!'

The sun is streaming onto the verandah, highlighting the freckles on Mr Hennessy's face. Noah reaches behind his chair and picks up a large white sun hat. He carefully places it on his dad's head.

'If it gets too hot, me and Darcy will bring you inside.'

We walk down a long hallway of polished wooden floorboards. There are no mats anywhere in the house and most of the furniture is pushed against the walls. To get the wheelchair around?

'Where's your mum?'

Noah walks into the kitchen and opens the fridge. He takes out a bottle of Coke and pours two glasses, watching the froth almost overflow before topping them up.

'I don't know.' His voice is quiet. 'She has trouble staying on the right side of hope.'

He glances down the hallway, as if his dad could wheel himself in at any moment.

I ask, 'How about you?'

'Me?' He swallows hard. 'I just want Dad to be normal again. That's not so bad, is it?'

I shake my head and drink the Coke, quickly. The

gas burns as it goes down, making me burp loudly.

Noah laughs. 'Good comeback, Walker.'

We both look at the photo on the fridge door. It's of the three of them, at the beach. A young Noah sits near his dad, who's handing him a slice of watermelon in the shape of a smile. Noah's mum is leaning forward, the juice dribbling down her chin.

Noah says, 'Me and Dad would dig a hole in the sand and he'd draw a line with his toe, a metre away. We'd have a competition to see who could spit the most pips into the hole.' Noah's voice catches in his throat. 'He'd let me win.'

A few tears roll down his cheeks. He stares at the photo. With one finger he reaches out to touch his father's image.

I put my hands in my pockets and wait, feeling as useless and tongue-tied and frustrated and uncertain and scared as his dad must be, sitting alone out there on the verandah.

What would a real man do in this situation? Hug him? Put an arm around his shoulder? Pat him on the back? Say, 'Cheer up, Noah.'

God, what's a real man anyway?

I walk across the kitchen and wrap my arms around Noah. He sobs quietly. We stand like this for a few minutes, not moving. The photo watches us mutely from the fridge.

'When my family went to the beach, Dad would kick a plastic soccer ball towards me and I'd watch it roll by, hoping the wind would blow it into the water. Stupid ball!'

Noah giggles and steps back, wiping his eyes. 'Sorry, Darcy.'

He takes the hankie out of his pocket and blows his nose loudly.

'No worries, Hennessy. Just wait until I tell Tim tomorrow!'

Noah laughs. 'He's scared of a plastic snake!'

We walk out to the verandah together. Noah stops before the door and looks towards his dad.

He whispers, 'Nothing at school worries me anymore.'

We play chess for the next hour, this time with Mr Hennessy on my side. To make Noah feel better, I ask his dad for advice, pretending he's involved. After a while I begin to notice little things, the flutter of his eyelashes when I make the wrong choice, the baleful stare when I make a really stupid crazy move, the flicker in his eyes when I choose well.

Maybe I'm imagining it? I study his face closely,

sure I can pick the subtle differences. Noah notices. His dad is with us. We even won a game!

After I say, 'Checkmate', I reach across and touch his father's arm.

It's warm and soft and fleshy.

And alive.

When it's time to leave, I kneel in front of Mr Hennessy. 'I hope me and you can play each other next time I visit, sir.'

Again I notice the change in his eyes.

I stand up and give Noah another hug.

'Don't try and hug me at school, Walker or I'll knee you in the crutch.'

'No worries, Noah. See you tomorrow.'

I walk slowly along his street. The wind haunts the leaves, but it isn't scary or mournful. It's melodic. The shadows of the trees dance along the footpath. The clouds definitely are television-commercial soft.

How close is too close?

'Audrey?'

'Mmm?'

'Why are men lousy at hugging each other?'

Audrey raises herself on one elbow and frowns.

'Not all men. My dad hugs Uncle Ted. A big slobbery embrace every Christmas to make up for not seeing him the rest of the year.'

We're stretched out on the soft grass under a tree in Bussellton Park, beside the stream. Fifty metres away is a playground where two girls chase each other around a wooden pirate ship. They climb slowly up to the front of the ship. The youngest girl stands near the skull-and-crossbones flag and spreads her arms wide. The other girl wraps her arms around her sister to stop her from falling. They both shout for their mum to watch. The mother claps her hands and laughs.

Audrey wriggles closer to me.

'You can hug me, if you want. To practise.'

'You're not a man, Audrey.'

She rests her head on my shoulder and I look through the leaves of the plane tree at the sky, thinking of Noah and his dad, thinking of how I wanted to hug his dad too. But it would seem really soppy or stupid or fatalist, as if I was admitting there was a problem.

'Are you still thinking of hugging men, Darcy?'

'Yep. Only one man though.'

'Who?'

'It's a secret.'

Audrey pokes me in the ribs, gently.

'I love secrets, tell me.'

'Do you know the definition of secret?'

'Yeah, sure. Information shared only between good friends.'

'Not quite.'

'Okay, I won't hassle you about this mysterious man you want to wrap your arms around.'

'It's not a sexual thing.'

'I thought we agreed not to mention the "S" word anymore?'

'Nah, that was last night. Today, we can indulge for as long as you want.'

Audrey checks her watch. 'Until six o'clock when I've got to be home.'

'So this is daylight sex?'

Audrey giggles. 'It's not sex. It's sex talk. Like those 1900 numbers you see advertised in magazines.'

'I've always wanted to ring one, just to listen. How erotic does it have to be for three dollars and thirty cents a minute? Does the woman swear, or just mention bodily parts? Or say something stupid like . . .' Audrey adopts a breathy fake voice, '"Take me, baby, take me . . . NOW!"'

I jump when she moans loudly. 'Geez, Audrey, you scared the hell out of me.'

Audrey pats my shoulder, reassuringly. 'Sorry, it looks like I'll never make it as a – whatever they're called.'

We both lie quietly for a few minutes, eyes closed, drifting away, our bodies touching, Audrey's breath on my face. I'm surprised I'm not a bundle of nerves.

How did we get here, so close, so quickly?

It was only last night when we kissed.

My blackhead hasn't even reached full bloom. Yet I'm comfortable hugging Audrey, girl of my dreams since Year Nine. The girl who thinks *Heart of Darkness* sucks shit big-time. The girl with the brown eyes and one patch of green. The girl who right now is – snoring beside me.

Well, breathing very heavily.

I dare not move. Pins and needles tingle down my shoulder to my elbow. One of the girls at the playground starts crying and runs to her mother. I try wiggling my fingers to get the blood moving. Audrey sighs in her sleep and I feel the rush of air tickle my nose. I concentrate on the tree above our heads, counting the branches, trying to guess how old it must be. Audrey moves her leg a little closer, wrapping tightly around me. Her eyes are closed and one hand is curled in a tight little fist under her chin. The other hand rests on my chest.

I'm trapped.

Any movement will wake her.

Her face is so near.

No blackheads.

No blemishes.

There is a fingernail mark under her left eye. It's so faint I can barely see it. I lean closer. Maybe she scratched herself while sleeping. A long wisp of hair curls along her cheek and falls near her mouth. I want to brush it away. I can see every hair follicle on her fringe. Her hair is ink black, even in the dappled sunlight.

And on her chin is . . .

'Hey!'

I reel back, rolling quickly away. My knees shake and my hands wave uncontrollably in front of me like a puppet on steroids.

Audrey sits up. 'You scared me!'

'I scared you!'

Audrey rubs her eyes.

'I was sleeping. I opened my eyes and you were . . .'

'I was looking at you. I know. I'm sorry. I thought you were asleep.'

'I was!'

'I didn't mean . . . I was looking at you . . . You were . . .'

'I was what?'

I can't say beautiful. I'd feel like a real prat.

An elderly couple walk along the path. The grey-haired man is dressed in shorts and long socks. His legs are blindingly white. His wife has a little terrier on a leash. The dog is sniffing in the bushes along the path, stopping every few seconds to wag its tail and explore.

Audrey repeats, 'I was what?'

She kneels in the grass, brushing her hair away from her face again. Maybe that's how she got the scratch.

'I'm sorry. I can't say. It's too embarrassing.'

'More embarrassing than condoms stuffed in a letterbox?'

'I was admiring you.'

'You were looking at me while I slept!'

'You fell asleep on my shoulder. I didn't know what else to do.'

'Except look at me.'

'Better than looking at the dog.'

As if on cue, the dog barks once and comes close, sniffing the ground near us.

Audrey reaches out to pat him. He barks again, turns and scampers back to the path and the old couple.

They smile at us.

Audrey waves.

She turns to me, deep in thought.

'Did you just compare me to a dog?'

I swallow hard.

'Unintentionally, yes.'

Audrey leaps up and jumps on me, knocking me backwards in surprise. We sprawl on the grass. Audrey pins my hands to the ground with her legs, sitting on my chest. She's smiling as she leans down and kisses me. Her hair tickles my face. In one quick movement, she rolls off me and resumes her position lying beside me, head near my shoulder. She whispers, 'If I fall asleep again, Darcy, look at the dog, okay!'

'I didn't mean . . .'

Audrey raises her fingers to my lips and whispers, 'Shhhh. You talk too much.'

I add, 'And don't say anything.'

Don't run with your shirt pulled over your face

Dad collects the ball near the half-way line, spins out of a clumsy tackle by the bald guy with the paunch, touches the ball forward while looking up, searching for a teammate. He sees the winger running fast – as fast as a forty-four-year-old ninety-kilo winger with a bad back and short legs can run.

Dad angles an exquisite thirty-metre diagonal ball over the defender's head, right into the path of the chubby winger as he cuts inside.

The winger attempts to control the ball on his chest but stumbles at the last moment. The ball bounces off his shoulder, hits the defender in the head and loops slowly out to the penalty area where Dad is following through.

Dad doesn't take his eyes off the ball and meets it on the volley.

He strikes it hard and low.

The ball flies towards goal, cannons off the knee of the goalkeeper, bounces across the goal, hits the post and then spins wickedly into the net.

Dad wheels away from the celebrating throng. He lifts his shirt over his head and runs along the touchline to where Audrey and me are cheering wildly.

He would have made it if someone hadn't left the first-aid kit too close to the line.

A sack of cabbages dropped from the back of a fast-moving truck has more elegance than Dad falling. But that doesn't wipe the grin from his face. He stumbles to his feet, a white powder line stained on his shorts, jersey and naked torso. As Dad is surrounded by excited teammates, he modestly pulls his shirt down. He trots back into position. Before the referee blows the whistle for the resumption of play, Dad looks across and gives me the thumbs up. I clap my hands above my head. I saw the crowd on television do that to Pele once. Audrey puts two fingers in her mouth and whistles at the top of her lungs. Dad waves again and then focuses on the game, chasing the ball across to the far side of the field.

Audrey leans close to me and whispers, 'Your dad's a great player, but he runs like a girl.'

The referee blows for half-time and Dad almost sprints off the field. He's breathing heavily by the time he reaches us, sweat dripping from his brow. He takes a long swig of water from the bottle I offer and smiles, 'One–nil. We've never beaten this team before.'

Audrey laughs, 'Maybe Darcy is your lucky charm, Mr Walker.'

Dad tips the rest of the water over his head. 'He'll have to come to every game now.'

He laughs to himself. 'Just kidding, son.'

He steps forward and gives me a sweaty, smelly football hug. 'Thanks for coming, Darcy.'

He hands me the empty water bottle and walks across to where his teammates are getting a pep talk from the coach.

Audrey punches me lightly on the shoulder.

'Looks like we have a football date for the rest of the season, Walker!'

I roll my eyes in mock horror.

****

I've got a new routine.

Each morning begins with the obligatory blackhead check and quick shower with facial scrub, followed by a hurried breakfast with one parent asking about Audrey.

'Yes, Mum we're still together. The sex is fantastic, particularly since we've ditched the condom. What do you think of the name *Othello* for a grandson?'

Mum is learning to ignore me. Dad still chokes on his toast, without fail. It's increasingly difficult dreaming up rude things to say this early in the morning. I told Audrey about it. She texts suggestions.

I get woken by the phone and dirty messages.

I walk to school via Noah's place. He's sitting on the verandah, waiting with his dad. In the past week, Mr Hennessy has started moving his fingers. Me and Noah sit and have one game of chess with his dad.

Whoever loses has Mr Hennessy as partner for the next day.

Me and Noah's dad have a system.

Fingers moving means good choice.

Thumbs moving means poor choice.

No movement at all means don't be so stupid.

At lunchtime, me and Audrey sit against the school fence, looking over the oval. Tim and Braith kick the ball to each other. Miranda, Stacey and Claire sit near the goalposts, watching the boys and laughing. Rumour has it that Claire is thinking of leaving school and moving in with butcher-boy. What some people will do for free meat!

After school, me and Audrey walk home across Bussellton Park, stopping at our spot under the plane tree. Sometimes we do homework in the shade. Sometimes we do other things, which aren't so boring.

****

My name is Darcy Franz Pele Walker. I have two weeks left in Year Eleven.

My best friend is Noah Hennessy.

My extra special best friend is Audrey Benitez.

And my dad is a great football player – for somebody of his age.

About the author

Steven Herrick was born in Brisbane, the youngest of seven children. At school his favourite subject was soccer, and he dreamed of football glory while he worked at various jobs. For the past twenty years he's been a full-time writer and regularly performs his work in schools throughout the world. Steven's work is both popular and critically acclaimed. His books have been shortlisted for the Children's Book Council of Australia Book of the Year Awards on six occasions and he has twice won prizes in the New South Wales Premier's Literary Awards with *by the river* and *the spangled drongo*. He lives in the Blue Mountains with his partner Cathie, a belly dance teacher, and their two sons, Jack and Joe. For more information, visit Steven at www.stevenherrick.com.au